In Time's Shadow

Amaranthine Vampires Trilogy
Book 2

TP Donohue

ISBN: 978-0-6459147-3-3 (eBook)

ISBN: 978-0-6459147-2-6 (paperback)

Editor: Lacey Braziel

Cover design: Victoria Cooper Design

Interior design and formatting: Cassie Weaver

Published in Australia by Wordfare Publishing

"The distinction between the past, present, and future is only a stubbornly persistent illusion."
Albert Einstein

Chapter 1

David

David studied his reflection in Essie's entryway mirror, straightening his tie as he held his phone to his ear with his shoulder. The day was not playing out as he imagined it. He had stopped by Essie's house to arrange the dinner date they had talked about before she left on holiday. He had almost talked himself out of the idea on the way over. He still wasn't convinced it was sensible for him to be part of her life. His world was risky and unpredictable. He didn't want to put her in danger. But he missed her while she was away. He missed her sharp eyes staring at him from behind her perpetually smudged glasses. He missed her knowing smile. And it was just dinner after all, wasn't it? But now, instead of making dinner plans, they were planning a journey to the past with Essie's long-dead mother to retrieve her father and hunt some Bloodborns.

Although it wasn't what he had anticipated, he didn't

mind the interruption. It meant he could put off answering the question of what his relationship with her was or should be for a little longer. And he had to go with her. There was no question. The Bloodborns had ended up in the past with Essie's father. They were a vampire problem which made it his problem.

The phone kept ringing. David sighed. No surprise. Raf was always mislaying his phone. He didn't care much for such modern conveniences. Essie's mother, Rhonda, said that Raf should go with them to the past. He had to admit that it would be reassuring if Raf was there. Despite his health problems, he was older and more experienced. And there was nothing he took more seriously than his vow to defeat the Bloodborns. Also, he would be furious with David, his younger sire, if he went after the Bloodborns alone. Still, he shifted his weight uneasily when Raf finally picked up the call.

He quickly updated him on the situation, then there was a long pause.

'I don't trust this Rhonda woman, *Dado*. How we know this is not trap of Bloodborns?' He spoke in broken English, accented by his Italian heritage.

David sighed. 'We don't I suppose. But what choice do we have?'

Raf grunted down the end of the line. David could almost hear the older man thinking and waited for what would come next.

'So, what about the dream you have?'

The dream. A shiver iced up David's neck, and he tried

to shake it off. In the past, his dreams had been a welcome experience. It was one reason he still slept, even though as an Amaranthine he didn't need sleep anymore. Memories came to him in dreams, vignettes from his long ago past.

After Raf had turned him, he went back home to see his family for the last time. Raf warned him against it. Better they think him dead since he could never tell them the truth. But he had gone anyway, lingering near the small village where he grew up. He stayed in the shadows as he followed them on the walk back to the Maric family home. Watching from outside the modest cabin, his heart ached as he saw them together, breaking bread for their evening supper. His mother's long, heavy plait hung over her shoulder when she leaned to serve the food. His sisters placed their napkins delicately in their laps.

But realising Raf was right, that there was nothing he could say to them that would make them understand, he took one last glance before he turned away and never went back.

And they were all gone now. Buried in a lonely cemetery near the village church. David didn't even have any pictures of them. The Marics had no money for photographs or sketches. Even if they did, his father would have frowned upon such wastefulness and vanity. Now his dreams were where he saw his mother and sisters, sometimes even his father. He had always welcomed those fleeting night-time glimpses of his life before, even if for just a moment.

Then early one morning, while Essie was away in

Greece, he had awoken with a start, pulling in gasps of air, as if all the oxygen had been sucked out of his bedroom. His heart raced and sweat beaded across his forehead. The images that had filtered up in his unconscious defied description. Amaranthine vampires – many hereditary pairs like him and Rafael – tortured, gutted, and beheaded. Their bodies lay discarded, mounded in a broken pile, and a dark, hooded figure stood over them. Blood ran unceasingly from the corpses, pooling on the floor. A horrific tableau. But it was the dream's end that haunted him the most. The first time he had the dream he thought it was an aberration. Now, every time he tried to sleep, the visions assailed him, completely overtaking the pleasant memories and darkening his sleep.

'Perhaps it is warning,' Raf had said, when David finally shared the dream with him, although he had not been able to talk about the dream's ending. But a warning about what? The Amaranthine had to be scarce in numbers now. He and Raf had not come across another like them for over a century. At first Raf said it wasn't that unusual. Time had a different meaning for them. The passage of decades could feel momentary. And the Amaranthine lived largely solitary existences, save for if they had a hereditary mate. It was safer that way. It attracted less attention from the humans. But lately, even Raf had begun to speculate if the two of them might be the last.

Yet there were a multitude of Amaranthine bodies in the dream. Pair upon pair. And the hooded figure stood triumphantly over them all. David never saw the figure's face, but somehow, he felt the figure was smiling, gleeful.

He shook himself, shifting the phone to his other ear. 'It's just a dream, Raf. I don't think it means anything.'

Raf tutted on the end of the line. 'All right. Answer another question. Do you go to past to deal with Bloodborns, or because Essie asks?'

David laughed. 'She didn't ask, Raf. She actually told me not to come. I insisted I should go. It could be dangerous. She needs protection.'

The older vampire sighed. 'She is mortal, *Dado*. You cannot protect her forever.'

He didn't know how to respond to that. He didn't know what to tell himself, let alone what to say that would convince his friend. The only word he could use to describe his feelings for Essie was conflicted. But even that didn't seem adequate. And he had no idea how she felt about him. At length, Raf exhaled, relenting.

'Where we meet?'

He smiled to himself. 'I'm at Essie's house. Meet us here.'

Raf grunted. 'I bring supplies. We feed before we leave.'

As he ended the call, David realised he didn't even know what 'leaving' would mean. What were the mechanics of time travel? How would they be transported to the past?

A scent washed over him. The high note was lavender, but there were hints of sweet cloves as well, like Essie. He turned to find Rhonda standing in the entryway with him. In the flesh, he could see that mother and daughter were similar and yet different. Essie's blue eyes had come from Gilbert, since Rhonda's were a pale green. Her dark hair contrasted Essie's lighter colour. But the corners of their mouths turned up in the same way, and they both tilted their heads to the side when they were concentrating.

'You'll need to leave that here.' She pointed at his mobile phone. 'We don't have those where I come from. The future Essie warned me not to dabble with technology. She also told me to make sure we don't bring anything back with us. She specifically said you and Rafael shouldn't try to bring any weapons. They can't pass through the wormhole. I was meant to tell you that.'

He nodded as he placed the phone carefully on the entry table and emptied his pockets of his keys and notepad. 'I don't have any weapons on me right now anyway, and I'll be sure to tell Raf.'

They went back into the lounge room as Essie was coming down the stairs. She had showered and changed into a fresh set of clothes. Her hair was wound in a wet knot at the back of her head and her glasses were slightly askew. He watched her descend the rest of the stairs. A warm, almost electric feeling surged through him. He knew he was staring but he couldn't drag his gaze away. Shaking himself, he adjusted his collar.

Rhonda's face lit up as Essie reached the bottom of the stairs. 'Look at you, Essie, so grown up. I can still hardly believe my eyes.'

Essie smiled at her mother tentatively. Her reaction to Rhonda's arrival had been, justifiably, cautious. It wasn't every day your dead mother turned up on your doorstep. And her uncertainty was still palpable in the look she gave Rhonda.

'Mum, I have a few concerns with your plan. The last time I opened a wormhole, I nearly destroyed a church and sucked half the city in with it. How do I know that won't happen again? And how do we control the destination?'

Rhonda held out her wrist to them, showing a white, matte-finish bracelet that resembled a fitness tracker.

'You solved all those problems, Ess. Well, the future you will solve them. We can travel using this.' She reached out to touch the bracelet. It lit up. Her eyebrows knit together in concentration.

'You called it the Time Weaver.'

Essie arched an eyebrow at her mother. 'That doesn't sound like a name I would use. It's so . . . abstract.' She held her mother's wrist carefully, inspecting the bracelet. 'But how did I miniaturise the technology? And stabilise the gravitational force?'

David peered over Essie's shoulder to see the Time Weaver. He didn't understand the science the way she did, of course, but in the church when they had fought Sabine, there were giant magnets that formed part of a temporal radiometer which was powering the wormhole. The setup was huge and had drawn on an enormous amount of energy. It seemed impossible all of that could be contained in a tiny wrist band, no bigger than a watch.

'I don't know how exactly,' Rhonda said apologetically. 'You tried to explain it to me, but . . . it's complicated. The important thing is you do figure it out. You also work out how to control the travel destination – mostly.'

Essie shook her head slowly. 'When do I do this? And why didn't the future me just go and get Dad from your time instead? Or why not come here to see me herself? Why did she send *you* to get me?'

Rhonda looked thoughtful as she lightly touched the bracelet, causing the light to power off. 'You were worried your dad would freak out if the future version of you came to get him and that he wouldn't listen to her.'

Essie chuckled lightly. 'How far in the future did I come from to see you? Did I look so old and wrinkled Dad wouldn't recognise me?' She brushed some stray hair out of her face self-consciously.

'There are rules,' Rhonda said. 'I'll explain that in a minute. But this version of you, now, is the one your father saw most recently, in the church. It will make it easier for him to accept that he needs to return here, to his present.'

David tried to picture Essie in ten or twenty years, her hair slowly fading to grey, her face softened and lined with age. Would she take more after Gilbert or Rhonda as the years passed by? The vision of an older Essie spurred a long-suppressed ache inside him. Growing old was something he would never get to experience, let alone growing old with someone else. It was one of the many human things he had been forced to give up. He pushed the thought away and cleared his throat.

'Rhonda, did the future Essie say anything about how we find Gilbert and the Bloodborns in the past?'

Rhonda turned her attention to him, nodding. 'I'm supposed to explain that when we get there. But before we leave, we need to go over the ground rules. There are three rules for time travel. They must be obeyed, no matter what.' She locked eyes with Essie. 'You made me memorise them.'

'Okay. What are the rules?'

Rhonda held up her index finger.

'First rule: You cannot time travel to the same place twice. You explained that time is like a delicate web. If you put too much pressure on the same thread, the web is weakened and will eventually snap. So this must be a one-off visit.'

Essie nodded. 'Okay.'

'Second rule: You can't interact with your past selves. Again, time is a delicate web. That kind of thing could snap the thread.'

'Well, that probably explains why the future Essie didn't come to see me.'

Rhonda nodded. 'And third rule: You must not change past events. No matter how tempted you are. This could destroy the web of time completely.'

David rubbed his chin as he contemplated the instructions. The analogy of time as a web was discomforting, both in its implied fragility and in how much it made it sound like they were heading into a trap.

Essie crossed her arms over her chest sullenly. 'But what does that mean – don't change past events? How do we stop events from changing? Just by going to the past we could change things.'

Rhonda's shoulders lifted in a slight shrug. 'The future Essie said that you would understand what it meant when you got there.'

Essie huffed. 'You know, Mum, future Essie seems quite cryptic.'

He had to agree with that. So far, they had little concrete information and the whole plan seemed unnecessarily convoluted. Moffatt appeared at Essie's feet and rubbed his long body against her leg as he purred. Essie's adopted cat had taken to him a little while she was away, even letting him pat him on one or two occasions when he had come over to feed and check on him. Essie reached down to scratch behind his ear.

'What about Moffatt? I'll need to get another cat sitter. And what about my job? The new semester starts in a few days. And there's a ball I'm supposed to attend. The Institute's going to announce a scholarship in honour of my friend, Cecil. He . . . he died recently.' She clasped the chain around her neck. It held a gold bicycle charm. She always wore it – a final gift from Cecil.

Rhonda patted the band on her wrist. 'You don't need to worry about any of that. Although the location can still be off a bit, no matter how long we are gone, you can return at the exact moment we leave. No time will have passed here at all. Moffatt won't even know you were gone, and you'll be back to start the semester.'

Essie looked to him again, her face ambivalent. He smiled, trying to hide his own concern. He was convinced it was the right thing for them to go. They also had little other choice. Yet there were many unknowns. For a start, where were they going? What if they weren't successful in bringing Gilbert back? What if they couldn't find the Bloodborns or they were already wreaking havoc in the past? What if something went wrong and they were stuck there indefinitely?

A sharp knock dragged their collective attention to the front door. Essie stepped past her mother to open it.

Raf stood there waiting, his face edged with a serious expression and a duffle bag slung over his shoulder.

'Hi, Rafael. Thanks for coming. Let me introduce you to my mother.'

Chapter 2

Essie

Essie fidgeted with her necklace as they sat together in the lounge room and her mother went over the plan again.

Her mother.

It sounded so strange. She was still getting over seeing her again, alive and well, thanks to the magic of time travel. The same lines she remembered crinkled at the edges of her eyes when she smiled. The same layers of wooden beads adorned her neck. Looking at her stole Essie's breath. She had to keep reminding herself that she was real. And yet, there was no time to dwell on that.

The plan was straightforward. Her father, who she had also thought dead, was alive sometime in the past. Future Essie's instructions were to find him and bring him back. That made sense to her. Leaving her father in the past could spell disaster. Paradoxes and time loops made for interesting plots in science fiction books and movies, but the reality was yet to be explored – let alone solved. Who knew what impact it could have if two versions of the same person existed at the same time from different points in history?

But he was also the father who had betrayed her. In that cold stone church, he had allied himself with a bloodthirsty vampire as part of a plan to prevent the car accident that would claim her mother's life. She wasn't sure how she felt about seeing him again now.

Then there was the problem of the Bloodborns. David and Rafael were adamant they needed to deal with them too.

'They are young ones, untrained. They are not great physical threat to me and *Dado*,' Rafael told her in his accented English. 'But they are more unpredictable. Hungrier. There is no one like Sabine to rein them in now.'

She nodded at him, but a feeling of unease slid over her. Still, how hard could it be?

Find Dad.

Kill Bloodborns.

Easy, right?

She swallowed past the dry lump in her throat. Her mother stood up and beckoned them to join her in the middle of the lounge room.

'We all need to be physically connected for the Time Weaver to transport us,' she explained. Rafael grumbled softly as he got to his feet. Everything was moving so quickly. She wanted more time. Time to think and tease out all the possibilities. To make contingency plans. To just take a breath.

David grasped her hand and gave it a gentle squeeze.

At least he was coming with her. She tried to focus on his reassuring touch and ignore the knot in her stomach as it wound tighter. Her mother pressed a few buttons on the Time Weaver, and a blue light appeared around them like mist, enveloping them and spreading through the lounge room. Her mother took hold of her free hand and then reached for Rafael's as the four of them made a small circle.

'Try to relax,' her mother said. 'It makes it easier.'

Essie locked eyes with David as the mist spread. His face was calm, his air confident. She envied him. If she didn't understand so much about quantum physics, she imagined it would be a lot easier to just close her eyes and hope for the best. But she did understand. The number of mathematical variables, the problems with the original code she had designed, all the kinks yet to be tested and smoothed out – these were apparently things she would solve one day. But it was hard to trust someone you had never met, harder still when that person was one's future self. Whoever that version of her was, the woman she would become, she was years away.

The blue mist grew brighter, drifting up to her shoulder height, and the familiar surrounds of her lounge room – the couch, the worn carpet – all began to fade. The light morphed into a circular rainbow. It spun around them like a hula hoop, gathering momentum by the second. The circle's slipstream started lifting her hair. Papers lying on the coffee table floated gently into the air. Her chest tightened as she recalled the destruction the wormhole had wreaked on the church, heavy wooden pews and slate tiles sucked up and away as if they were made of tissue. But as the wind gently increased, her couch and coffee table remained in place. A roaring sound whirred around them, pouring through her ears.

Her mother's eyes were closed and she breathed steadily even as her hair whipped back and forth across her face. The rainbow spun and spun, until the light grew so bright, she too had to squeeze her eyes shut to keep it out. The skin on her scarred hand tingled and a sensation of sinking overtook her. She reflexively sucked in a deep breath while her chest seized, as if she were being wrenched backwards by an invisible wire anchored somewhere in her core. Echoes of familiar voices reached her ear through a dull, reverberating shudder. The ground beneath her seemed to tilt away, as if she were cresting a rollercoaster at its highest peak, just about to plunge down. David's hand in hers was the only thing that felt real. It gave her the courage to lean forwards. She let go of her breath and fell slowly. Eventually her feet touched down, first her tiptoes, then her heels finding the solid earth beneath, as the shuddering stopped.

The light around her faded to black, and she tentatively opened her eyes. The world began to reappear around her, solidifying and taking shape.

Rafael immediately dropped her mother's hand and shook himself, flexing his fingers. Essie made a mental inventory of her body, finding everything still in one piece. David checked their surrounds before releasing her. She shivered at the sudden lack of warmth and the cooler air. They had left in bright daylight and arrived in darkness. It looked like they were in the middle of a narrow alleyway between tall buildings. Cars bustled behind them and the smell of garbage filled her nostrils.

Her mother held up her wrist and peered at the face of the Time Weaver.

'We've arrived at the right time. Now we just need to get to the right place.'

'What do you mean?' Essie asked, as she turned slowly, trying to orient herself. It wasn't any good. She did not recognise the alley at all. They could have been anywhere.

'We're downtown somewhere,' David said.

'Like I was saying before we left, the time destination is accurate, but the location can be a bit off target.'

Essie nodded as she tried to think what might have caused the problem with wayward locations. She made a mental note to examine it later.

'So, *when* are we then, exactly?'

'Let's find a train station.' Her mother headed off, seeming to ignore her question. She walked in the direction of the cross street at the end of the alley.

'Why we going on train?' Essie recognised the air of suspicion in Rafael's voice and her brows knitted together. Her mother turned around and smiled at him.

'You know, you're exactly how the future Essie described you.'

Rafael folded his arms over his chest, unwilling to move without an answer.

'We're going to the last stop.' Her mother's face creased with a smile and Essie's heart jumped with recognition. She took several quick steps to keep pace.

The last stop!

It was a song they used to sing when they were on their way home on the train from a day spent out in the city. Her mother had made up a tune to help her remember the directions home, so that if she ever got lost, she would know how to find her way back. Get on the train and go all the way to the last stop. All the way home.

'The last stop is in Feldham. It's the town where I grew up.'

Her mother answered with a wide smile as she led them out of the laneway and into the brightly lit street. A handful of cars passed by as they walked a few blocks.

'There,' David said, pointing. They crossed to a set of stairs leading down into the station. Laughter rang out as a group of grungy teenagers passed them. At the bottom of the steps, a couple toting suitcases on wheels and wearing matching backpacks stood beside each other poring over a city network map. Her mother stopped, fished around in her pockets, and withdrew a handful of gold coins.

'I don't suppose any of you have any money on you?' She indicated towards the ticket booth sign that said cash only. 'I should have thought ahead.'

Essie knew she wasn't carrying any money. She hardly ever did anymore with all the electronic options. David patted his pockets and also came up empty, except for his customary handkerchief and silver watch.

'I'll get the tickets,' Rafael said, vanishing. She raised her eyebrows at David, but he only shrugged in response. As they walked slowly past the ticket booth, the seller eyed them up and down briefly. On the other side of the booth,

Rafael reappeared, and once they were out of view, he flourished four train tickets in his palm.

Her mother took her ticket gratefully and motioned them onwards.

'The line to Feldham leaves from that platform.' She pointed to the back of the station. As they walked, Essie glanced between the schedules posted at each platform and the large art déco analogue clock mounted back near the station entrance. It was almost 9.00 p.m., and according to the schedule, the last train for the Feldham line would arrive shortly. David took out his silver pocket watch and adjusted the hands to match the large clock.

They waited on the platform, and Essie tried to think through their next steps.

'So, when exactly will our version of Dad arrive? Or is he here already?'

Her mother hesitated, twirling her beads between her fingertips.

'I'm not completely sure.' She stretched onto her toes to peer down the track, searching for the coming train. 'You only said that he wouldn't come to the house. You said I should take you to Feldham and leave you there. After that, it was up to you.'

The train whooshed into the station, wafting Essie's hair away from her face. The doors slid open with a hiss and David and Rafael waited as they stepped in. Her mother moved down the aisle until she reached a set of vacant seats facing each other. Essie sat down next to her while David folded himself into the window seat and Rafael slid in beside him. A few more passengers straggled on before the doors closed and the train moved off. Essie stole a glance at her mother and resisted the urge to keep staring. Most of her mental images of her were distorted by time and memory. When she looked at her now, the walking and talking version of her, it was too surreal. What did she think of her, her grown daughter? How long would she get to spend with her? Did she know what would happen to her one day? Did she know that a stupid car accident would claim her life? She tried to push those thoughts aside and refocus on the reason they were all here. Her eyes flitted to David as he cleared his throat.

'Before we left, you were saying the two versions of Gilbert Thornton – they can't both be in the same place at the same time?'

Her mother nodded. 'The future Essie explained it to me. Or she tried to. It was very technical, especially for me. I'm a library assistant, not a physicist.' She smiled. 'But you were very clear. When you find your dad, you have to convince him to return to the future with you before he causes any trouble.'

A bubble of anger formed in her chest, but she bit back a response as David caught her eye, his face apprehensive. *Before he causes any trouble.*

It was a bit late for that. Her father had already betrayed her, joined forces with an ancient clan of vampires, and almost got Rafael and David killed.

But her mother didn't seem to know about what her father had done in the present, and even without a warning look from David, she instinctively felt she should keep that knowledge to herself. Although maybe her mother could explain it to her, help her understand why he did it. After all, he said it was all for her. She forced herself to refocus.

'So where are *your* Gilbert and well . . . me . . . the younger me, I mean?'

Her mother shifted uncomfortably. 'They're at home. They think I went out to buy milk.' She hesitated. 'I didn't want to lie to them, but you told me I couldn't tell them about any of this. You said it was important they never know you were here. And I trust what you said, what you asked of me.'

Essie worried her lip with her front teeth. Her mother trusted the future Essie. But could she trust her? It was an utterly bizarre situation to put her mother in. Why would her future self come up with *this* plan? Surely there had to be another way. Sighing, she leaned her head against the cool glass of the window.

She sensed David's eyes resting on her as the train picked up speed. Gradually, the brightly lit urban centre receded. Though darkness blanketed the landscape, she knew from memory that the scenery would soon give way to fence-lined paddocks and rolling hills. The train made three more stops with passengers boarding and disembarking. It stopped once more at Mount Major, then a voice over the loudspeaker announced Feldham Station as the next and final station on the line. The four of them stood up and made their way towards the exit.

The train halted, and Essie stepped out onto the platform. Everything she saw – the little station ticket booth, the painted signs and wooden bench seating, enveloped her in a string of moments from her childhood. She caught David and Rafael exchanging a strange look, and the memories evaporated.

'Do you feel that?' David asked.

'Hmm,' Rafael acknowledged.

'What is it?' She glanced around them. Everything seemed fine to her.

David touched his forehead, his face folding into a grimace. 'It's as if the air around us is vibrating.'

She halted, reaching out with her senses. 'Maybe it's some kind of atmospheric disturbance, like a low-pressure system coming through before a storm?'

She looked at her mother, but her mother only shrugged. 'I don't know. I didn't check the weather this morning.'

'*Dado*, we should go.' Rafael's voice was urgent. She glanced at him, his grey-streaked curls glinting in the moonlight, his keen eyes roaming the surrounds. What was he so worried about? Had he seen something? Could the Bloodborn vampires be lurking in the shadows? How could they have known to be at the train station at this moment?

There was a hand at her elbow and David steered her towards the platform exit behind her mother, who was leading the way.

'There's a motel about half a kilometre up this road. You can stay there tonight.'

The vampires remained tense, Rafael's eyes scanning the darkness periodically while David gripped her elbow. Her eyes drifted to her mother walking in front of her. The dichotomy of being home with her mother, contrasted with the peculiar circumstances of their reunion, struck a discordant note in her. It seemed as though the past and present were colliding all at once, leaving her in a hazy, dreamlike state. Was she hallucinating all of this? As they emerged onto the street near the station, she tried to make out other landmarks that would help reorient herself. Something just didn't feel right. She needed more details and facts. She needed evidence that all of this was real.

'Mum,' she said, slowing her pace. 'You said you would tell us the date once we arrived. So, when are we, exactly?'

'Oh, yes,' her mother answered over her shoulder. 'I can tell you now. Today is January sixteenth. It's exactly one month until your ninth birthday. Isn't that a funny coincidence?'

Essie's stomach contracted and lurched. She inhaled a sharp breath before keening into David's side.

It couldn't be.

It can't be.

She had forgotten a lot of things about her childhood, deliberately consigning them to the recesses of her mind. But she remembered that day, her ninth birthday, in vivid detail. It was the saddest, loneliest birthday she would ever have. After that, nothing would ever be the same again. Because her ninth birthday would be the first birthday without *her*. Because January sixteenth was only two days before the car accident that would claim her mother's life.

Chapter 3

David

David didn't hear what Essie and her mother were discussing. The loud noise in his head distracted him too much to notice anything else. It vibrated through him like a mortar shell leaving the canon. He struggled to focus over the sound as they walked towards the motel.

'*Dado*?' Raf questioned him in a tone too low for the others to hear.

'It's the drumming . . . can't you hear it?' he replied.

Raf gave a slight shake of his head.

Thankfully, Essie and her mother also seemed fine. Except now that he was paying attention, he could hear Essie's heart beating much faster. She dropped back to walk in step with him and leaned in, whispering.

'I have to tell you something.'

While Rhonda and Raf kept walking, Essie tugged his elbow, bringing him to a stop beside her.

'Today's date. Mum said its January sixteenth. The car

accident – it happens in two days, David. The date of the accident was January eighteenth.'

'You're sure? How can you know it's this year? Whatever year it is?'

She nodded. 'I'm sure. She said I'm turning nine in one month. The accident happened just before my ninth birthday.'

Oh no.

The drumming noise grew louder and bloomed into a burning sensation. He grimaced against the pain.

Two days until the car accident. Two days until Rhonda would die.

The future Essie's instructions about not changing past events rang in his ears.

You will understand what it means when you get there.

Raf turned and gave him a quizzical look. His sharp hearing had obviously caught the conversation. Realising they had all stopped walking, Rhonda also turned around to check on her daughter.

'Are you okay, sweetheart? It's not much farther.'

Essie straightened up, leaning away from him. He met her eyes with a cautioning look. She could not tell her mother what she knew. Not until they had thought it all through.

Remember the rules.

She swallowed. 'Yes, Mum. Coming.'

They continued along the main street towards the motel in silence. Feldham seemed like other small Australian country towns he had been to over the decades since immigrating and he didn't remember if he had visited it before. He was stationed in Mount Major, a bigger town thirty or so minutes down the freeway, back towards the city. They passed a small independent grocer and a petrol station, both closed for the day. There was a smattering of other tired looking shops, some with 'for lease' signs on the doors, the windows covered in sheets of old newspapers.

Some of the tension left his neck as Rhonda led them around a corner and stopped at the driveway to a small motel with a painted sign that read: 'The Homestead.' Pink neon lights flashed over the reception door indicating there were vacancies.

'They should have a room booked for me.' They waited outside as Rhonda went in and spoke to the man at the counter. Essie stood beside David, tight-lipped. He was relieved that whatever she was thinking, she had decided to wait until they were alone. Raf scanned their surrounds repeatedly. Despite David's initial misgivings about him coming along, he was glad that Raf was there. It was difficult keeping an eye out for danger while he was trying to ignore the persistent pressure in his head. He touched his temple gingerly, wondering what on earth could have brought it on.

'This way.' Rhonda returned with a room key, leading them past a row of shabbily painted doors, stopping in front of one with a brass number '12' nailed crookedly to it. The door opened to reveal a sparse looking room with shaggy carpet. There was a double bed covered in a quilted brown bedspread, a dresser, and a mini fridge in the corner. He could see an ensuite bathroom at the back.

Rhonda ushered them in and closed the door.

'It's basic, I know, but the best I could do in the situation. I wasn't really prepared for this.'

Of course not. Who is prepared for something like this?

Essie plonked down on the bed and the mattress dipped under her slight weight.

'This will be fine mum.' She wriggled forwards so her legs dangled over the edge.

'How are you feeling now, David?' Rhonda asked.

'Fine, thanks.' He stole a glance at Raf.

'So what is plan then? We hide here until old man show his face? Or we go hunt him and Bloodborns?'

Essie bristled, and David couldn't tell if Raf's choice of words had been deliberate or a product of the older vampire's muddled English. Rhonda seemed amused rather than annoyed. She placed the room key on the dresser.

'I'm sorry, but the future Essie didn't give me a lot of details about what happens next. She explained it was better that way. My job was to find you and bring you here safely, then go back to my life again as usual and not speak of this to anyone. But she said this would help.'

She pulled out a piece of heavy looking paper from her pocket and handed it to Essie. As she unfolded it, a smile broke out across her face.

'It's an old menu from *La Fortuna*. Dad's first restaurant.'

Her mother nodded. 'There's a phrase written on it too, on the other side.'

Essie flipped it over and smoothed it out on her lap. In

the margin, scrawled in what looked to be Essie's own messy hand, there were the words '*The absence will reveal the presence.*'

'I don't know what that means or how it will help, but I was meant to give it to you.' Rhonda's mouth lifted in a half smile as she pulled the folds of her cardigan together. A moment passed in silence, then her face fell.

'I'm supposed to go home now. Tomorrow, I'll be at the library as usual, like nothing happened.'

Essie laid the menu on the bed and stood up, reaching for her mother's hand.

'Mum, what else did the other Essie say? Did she say anything about . . . about the future, about *your* future?'

David tensed, sending her a warning glance.

Rhonda shook her head and shrugged. 'No. You said it was too risky for me to know anything about my own future. But you did say that I don't need to worry because everything would be okay.'

Essie bit down on her lip as she narrowed her eyes. They had only been in the past a few hours but the look on her face told him she was already contemplating breaking the most important rule they had been given.

You must not change past events.

Frustration and concern flared in his chest. The future Essie had to have known how hard that would be for herself to do. How could she have known what was to come, in barely a few days, and expected herself to walk away?

Rhonda stood back and smiled at her daughter, her eyes shining.

'Anyway, I don't need you to tell me my future, darling. I can already see it, right now, in front of me – my beautiful grown-up daughter.' She squeezed Essie's hands. 'You are everything that I always imagined you'd be. It will be so hard going home now and keeping all this a secret. But you told me that was how it had to be. And I promised you – the future you – I would do as you asked.'

'You could stay a bit longer.' She held mother's hands firmly. 'You could tell me a story, like you used to, when I was little.'

Rhonda smiled. 'Oh, you do love your stories. And I'd love to stay longer, but I think we should do what you told us to. There will be plenty more time for stories.'

David's heart clenched, and he exchanged a glance with Raf.

No, there won't.

There won't be any more stories.

You won't ever see her again.

Essie opened her mouth to speak but quickly fell silent. Rhonda didn't seem to notice as she buttoned her cardigan and reached for the door handle.

'Oh, I nearly forgot!' Pulling up her sleeve, she slipped off the Time Weaver and pressed a button on the side before passing it to Essie.

'You'll need this when you find your father, to take you all back to the future. I've reset it so once you put it on, it will be biologically coded to you. You'll be the only one who can use it.' She leaned over Essie for a moment, explaining how to adjust the settings for the time and destination. Essie took the band from her mother and carefully wrapped it around her wrist.

'Okay, I should go.'

Essie's face crumpled, and he watched, helpless to do anything.

'Thank you both for what you are doing for my daughter.' She nodded at him and Raf. He smiled tightly at her while Raf gave her a curt tilt of his head. Then she took Essie in her arms, holding her tightly.

'Goodbye, for now, my darling.'

As she reached for the door handle, Essie grasped her hand again.

'Wait, Mum . . . there's something I should tell you . . .'

Between one of Essie's heartbeats and the next, he was at her side. He took her gently by the arm as Rhonda turned around, her eyebrows drawn together.

Essie braced. She drew a breath, two breaths, as the silence extended.

'I . . . I love you, Mum. I'll always love you.'

'And I love you! My beautiful, amazing daughter.'

Essie's breath stilled as Rhonda leaned in and pressed a soft kiss to her cheek. Then the door scraped open, and she was gone. Essie stood on the threshold. Would she run after her? He didn't want to have to physically restrain her. But after a moment, her shoulders dropped, and she turned around. Kicking off her boots and removing her glasses, she slumped back on the saggy bed. His heart pressed in on him. He wanted to comfort her but wasn't sure how or if she would even want that from him. Staring straight ahead, she pressed her lips tightly together.

Somehow, she had kept the rules. Her own rules. And in doing so, she had held back the impossible weight of her knowledge and all that it meant.

It was Raf who broke the silence. 'It is late. You sleep, Essie.' His tone was softer than usual, almost tender.

She lay down and curled onto her side without acknowledging him.

'I'll take first shift, *Dado*.' Rafael gave him a meaningful look as he slipped out the door. The first shift. The first *watch*. They needed to be on their guard. There was the ever-present threat of the Bloodborns, leaderless and stranded in a strange place. They were loose cannons, displaced in time, and capable of anything. And as it was, he was no help. His head was still throbbing, and he couldn't tear his mind from Essie.

'Do you want to talk?' he asked, sitting down on the bed beside her.

'There's nothing to talk about.' She kept her eyes forwards, expressionless.

'Are you sure?' he pressed. 'It seems like a lot to take in. Suddenly you're here two days before the accident that killed your mother, but you can't do anything to change it.'

'It's fine,' she said flatly. 'We have to obey the rules. That all makes sense. Look what happened when my dad tried to change the past.'

'But that doesn't make it any easier to let go of this chance.'

He shuffled closer to her, but she rolled away, pulling herself into a tight ball with her back to him.

'It's just the way it has to be. I accept that. It can't be changed now. You heard the rules.'

David sighed. She seemed determined not to discuss it further. Maybe sleep would help. He reached for the blanket at the end of the bed and laid it carefully over her before turning off the overhead light. Pulling up a chair by the window, he loosened his tie and removed his suit jacket, draping it over the back of the chair. He took out the pocket watch from his waistcoat and flicked it open. It was later than he thought it would be. In several hours, a new day would dawn. His palm closed over the watch, and he held it, savouring the way it fitted perfectly in his hand, its reassuring weight. At least something was still the same. And tomorrow, they would find Essie's father. They would convince him to go home. Then at least one thing would be set right.

Chapter 4

Essie

Essie's eyes fluttered open in the dark of the motel room. There seemed little point forcing them closed any longer, hoping restlessly that sleep would find her. The garish red numbers on the bedside clock told her it was 4:00 a.m.

Her arms and legs protested as she unfurled them, and her mouth felt dry. Would the motel bathroom have a complimentary toothbrush? David's figure was silhouetted against the sheer motel curtains. He reminded her of a sentinel, silent and still. His jacket was off, his waistcoat unbuttoned, and shirt sleeves rolled up.

She flinched when he suddenly leaned towards her, resting his elbows on his knees.

'Sorry, I didn't mean to scare you. Can't sleep?' His voice was raspy.

She brushed a few loose strands of hair out of her eyes and sat up against the headboard.

'Is it the lumpy pillows? Or is the mattress too soft?'

He passed her the pair of glasses she had discarded on the bedside table earlier.

'It's not the bed. Well, it's not *only* the bed.'

How could she logically articulate everything going on inside her when all of it was confusing? He kept his eyes steady, waiting.

'It's just, nothing makes sense.'

'What do you mean?'

Her muscles tensed and she scrunched her hands into balls.

'I don't understand why I would put myself through this. Why would future me send my mother to bring us back here, to this very moment, to get my father? Why would she dangle the possibility of saving her in front of me while at the same time telling me I cannot intervene?'

There was no hesitation in his answer.

'I can only assume you knew what you were doing.'

She let out a clipped laugh. 'But what if I'm wrong? What if the future me made a mistake? I could save her, for me and for my father. All we'd have to do is go and get her and . . . and take her away somewhere else, anywhere else.'

David sank back against the chair and folded his arms across his chest. His habit of remaining stoic in the face of her outbursts made her feel even madder at herself. She was meant to be the calm, rational one. But lately the rollercoaster of her emotions had taken over.

'In the church, when we fought Sabine, you told your father that sometimes we have to let go, that learning to live with the pain of loss is part of loving.'

Her stomach twisted with a pang. It was unfair to bring that up.

'Sabine was threatening to suck the world into a wormhole to get her hands on the time travel technology. This is different. I'm in control here.'

He inclined his head thoughtfully. 'Are you?'

She threw up her hands, sighing loudly. 'Of course I am. There has to be a logical solution to this problem, and I can find it.'

He tented his fingers and hesitated a moment before he spoke again. 'Sometimes logic points us in a direction our heart doesn't want to follow.'

'What do you mean?'

She could hear the emotion in her voice and hated it, but she was powerless to stop it.

'In all my time on this earth, I've never met anyone like you. I think you knew what you were doing sending us here. I have faith in you, both now *and* in the future, to figure this out.'

Her ego purred with his compliments. She couldn't help it. But honestly – faith?

Ugh.

She pressed her lips together tightly. He was trying to help. And maybe faith helped him because he grew up in another time. A time when faith meant something. But for her, faith was in the same bag as feelings. It was anathema to science. It couldn't be measured or tested. It was intangible and amorphous. Faith couldn't help her understand the physics of time travel, temporal distortions, and paradoxes. It couldn't show her the logical course of action. It certainly couldn't help her save her mother.

She took a breath before speaking, worried that as her temper flared, she might say something she'd regret.

'The science that I understand now tells me that my future self is right. Changing the past is a bad idea. There are too many variables and unknowns.'

He stood up and then the mattress shifted under his weight as he sat down on the bed next to her. Pulling her knees up to her chest, she tugged the edge of the blanket, twisting the fabric between her fingers.

'But your heart tells you something else, doesn't it?'

He met her eyes and held them, but she shook her head stubbornly.

'It doesn't matter what my heart says. I don't want to be like *him*. I won't abandon reason and everything I know to chase an emotion, a feeling.'

'Mmm,' he murmured. 'But it's hard to walk away from the chance to make things different. I understand. There are certainly things in my past I would change if I could.'

His gaze dropped away. She tried to see his face more clearly, but it was hard to make out his expression in the dark. She had always been curious about his Amaranthine nature, the chemistry of his biology, the impossibility of his existence. But with a sudden wrench of guilt, she realised they had been so entangled in her own family problems since she met him, she hadn't given much thought to his past, to his human family. His youthful appearance often made her forget he was over one hundred years old now. He had told her he was in his mid-thirties when he was turned. He must have had a life before then. A full life. She knew he had served in the army. But maybe he had had a wife or children of his own?

'Did you ever see your family after . . . after you became Amaranthine?'

He took a moment to answer. 'Once, briefly. But I didn't speak to them. It would have been too difficult. Rafael turned me at the end of the war. Many soldiers from my village did not return. My family thought I died or deserted, and it was better to leave it that way.'

She didn't need to ask him if he still missed them. It was clear from the wistful tone of his voice that he did.

'My father could be a difficult man too,' he continued. 'Our relationship was often strained.'

She raised her eyebrows at him.

David laughed lightly. 'No, he didn't nearly cause half a city to be sucked into a giant wormhole. But he disapproved of most of my decisions in life. He wanted me to marry and take over our family business. He was a carpenter. But I wanted to join up. When I left for the front, he refused to come and see me off and would not allow my mother or sisters to come either.'

Essie's heart panged as a vision of him came into her mind; dressed in a khaki uniform, standing alone on a train platform, heading off to the battlefront. It made sense to her he would enlist. He had a strong sense of honour. Surely his father knew that about him? She tried to imagine him with his mother and sisters. What would they have been like? Did they have his brown hair? Were they tall like him? Had there been anyone else he loved?

'Was there ever anyone special, over the years, besides your friendship with Rafael?'

As soon as she had blurted out the words, her cheeks began to burn. She wasn't surprised she said it. She had a knack for not thinking before she spoke. But she had no right to pry into his personal life. David had told her his secret because he had no choice. They had worked together to solve a mystery and defeat the Bloodborns. Now they were friends, but that was all. Anything more would be a bad idea. They were from such different worlds. But it was hard to reconcile that with the connection she always felt to him. Intangible, yet so visceral. She braced herself for his response to her question. When he chuckled lightly again, she almost gave an audible sigh.

'No, no one special. Relationships with humans are difficult for me, for obvious reasons. You're the first human to know my secret. And it's dangerous for you, too.'

Something warm stirred inside her.

The first to know his secret.

She was the first to know who he really was. He'd said something to her about that once. About how the thing we all long for is to really be seen by another person.

'What about you? Anyone special?'

Despite having asked him, she wasn't expecting the same question in return. Her face flushed again. Her dating history was short and full of embarrassing false starts. The whole idea left her nauseous with anxiety, so she had avoided it for the past few years.

'No one really,' she stammered. 'I've always been too busy, with my work.'

He nodded, and mercifully, didn't pursue the topic further. Her mind drifted back to what he had shared.

'I'm sorry you never saw them again, your family, I mean.'

He shrugged. 'It was a long time ago now. My memories of them have faded. But my subconscious must still have something buried in there somewhere. Things float to the surface in my dreams – a face, a feeling.'

Vampires dreamed?!

She sat up straight and leaned forwards. 'You dream?'

She knew that his physiology was still human in some ways – he breathed, his skin was warm to the touch, and his hair still grew. Maybe it wasn't that surprising that his brain function was still human in that way too. But where was the line between human and vampire drawn? There was still so much to learn about it. About him.

'Yes, it's one of the only reasons I still bother with sleep. Although I haven't slept so much lately.'

'Oh? Why did you stop?'

He turned his face away and brought one hand up to rub his right temple. He seemed to be trying to clear something from his head. 'I started dreaming about other things, things I didn't want to see.'

She wanted to ask another question, but he stood up abruptly, his body tense. A rush of cold air breezed past the bed and she recoiled.

'Raf.'

In the dim light, she could make out Rafael's form. She thought his lips were moving, although she couldn't hear his voice.

David glanced at her, but she still couldn't read his expression properly in the darkness.

'You're sure?' he asked aloud, as he unrolled his shirt sleeves and reached for his jacket.

She pushed the blanket off and swung her legs over the side of the bed.

'What? What's happened?' She located her shoes with her toes. 'Is it my father? The Bloodborns?'

David flicked the bedside light on, bringing a dull glow to the room. He straightened his tie, then hesitated. He was clearly weighing his words before he spoke again.

'Neither,' he finally said.

Essie's thoughts swirled as she tried to imagine what new threat may have arisen in the few hours she had slept. The vampires exchanged another look, and she felt her shoulders tense.

'What is it?' she demanded.

When David turned to her, his eyes were a pale lilac. It wasn't a colour she had seen them before.

'Raf caught a strange scent back at the railway station when we arrived, so he went to investigate.'

She looked at Rafael, but he was giving nothing away.

'And?'

'And the scent was not Bloodborn, nor your father's.'

David glanced at Rafael again, and she raised her eyebrows at him expectantly. What was with the drip feed of information? Why weren't they telling her?

'So, what was it?'

David ran his hand through his hair. 'He thinks it might have been Amaranthine.'

'It was Amaranthine,' Rafael said with a lift of his chin. 'I'm certain of it.'

'What? But how is that even possible? You said you hadn't seen others of your kind for many decades. Not even when you were working here twenty years ago.'

Rafael gave a non-committal shrug of his shoulders, his grey eyes glinting. A smile played across his lips. He hardly ever smiled.

'Apparently,' David said. 'We missed something.'

Chapter 5

David

David stroked the new stubble across his chin, grateful that the pressure in his head had eased off and he could concentrate properly again. He turned over the revelation of the other Amaranthine in his mind.

We are not the last after all.

Something about the idea of it was comforting. How long had he struggled with the solitude of his and Raf's existence? The knowledge that there may be some fellow voyagers on the great sea of time gave him a renewed sense of belonging. There were still others like them. Still holding on. Still keeping the vow. Raf certainly seemed buoyed by the idea. David had not seen him look so pleased about anything in a long while.

'Should we try to find them?' Essie asked. 'Will they help us?' She zipped up her boots.

Raf shook his head. 'No. We have mission here. We do not need help. They will find us when they want.'

'But why are they here at all? Why didn't you meet them when you were here before, the first time?'

Raf brushed a stray cobweb from the sleeve of his leather jacket and shrugged.

'I assume they come for the same reason as us – the Bloodborns.'

Essie looked to David with a sceptical expression. He pondered her questions further. Raf's answer made sense. Why else would the Amaranthine have come to a tiny country town? Hunting Bloodborns was what they did. Still, something was niggling at him. A feeling of unease bubbled up, although he couldn't articulate a reason for it. But Raf was also right about their mission. Their first priority was to locate Gilbert Thornton.

'I think we should focus on finding your father for now.'

For a moment, Essie stared at him, her mouth slightly open as if she were about to speak. She hesitated, and her shoulders sunk.

'All right,' she said. 'I just need to use the bathroom before we go.'

After the door to the ensuite had closed behind her, he turned to Raf.

'Is there something you aren't telling me about the Amaranthine?'

Raf spread his hands expansively. 'It has been long time, but I know what I sensed.'

'I believe you. But are you sure we shouldn't go after them? Perhaps they *could* help us.'

Raf gave an impatient shake of his head. 'Not yet. Let us find old man and Bloodborns first.'

'But aren't you curious about them? It's been so long.'

He twirled a piece of his silver-streaked beard between his thumb and forefinger.

'Even centuries ago, when there were more of our kind, we did not travel in groups. Is dangerous. We draw too much attention from the humans. And now . . . how you say . . . the clock is ticking?'

'Yes. The accident. It happens tomorrow.'

'Will this be problem?'

He sighed. 'I don't think so. She says she knows what she has to do.'

Raf grunted. 'Let's find old man and kill Bloodborns and go home – *pronto*.'

Although he was curious about the other Amaranthine, it did seem the safest course of action to follow the original plan.

'How is your head, *Dado*?'

He touched his temple reflexively.

'Better. It's stopped hurting.'

'Good.'

Raf crossed to the window. Pushing the curtain aside, he peered out. The faint glow of the dawning sun lit his stern features, softening them a little. He flexed his neck to one side and then the other.

'Get the doctor. We go.'

Chapter 6

Essie

E ssie came out of the bathroom frustrated. She had tried and failed to tidy her hair back into a ponytail, so it hung loose around her shoulders. David held up her jacket, and she pushed her arms through the sleeves. As he lifted her hair out from under the collar, his fingers brushed the back of her neck, and goosebumps spread across her skin.

'Thanks,' she breathed, turning to face him. He stared down at her for a moment and her thoughts drifted back to the conversation they had earlier. About his life before he was turned. About his family and his dreams.

She cleared her throat, and he stepped back.

'Raf's keen to get going,' he said, holding open the door for her.

As they left the motel room, she kept thinking about what it would be like to meet the other Amaranthine. What would they look like? Where did they come from, and what stories did they have to tell? Pondering those questions was a welcome distraction from thinking about seeing her father again.

A hot sensation gripped her chest whenever she thought of the moment he had appeared in the church at Sabine's side, revealing himself as her accomplice. He had done it because he couldn't let go. Acting on his selfish desire to have her mother back again, he had betrayed everything and everyone. Whatever happened, she would not end up like him. And if she had to accept her mother's loss, then so did he. She would find him and make him come home, no matter what.

David turned to her. 'Are you all right?'

How did he do that? He seemed to sense her unease even when she said nothing. But she didn't want to go over it all with him again. Not now. She pushed down her feelings and tried to smile.

'I'm fine. Let's go.' She grabbed the handle and pulled the motel door firmly closed.

Rafael shifted his weight restlessly while they handed over the key at reception before heading out to the driveway of the motel again.

David looked up and down the street.

'Can you think where your father might go if he suddenly found himself here, Essie? Where should we start?'

She reached into her pocket and pulled out the restaurant menu her mother had given her. She had no idea what the words written in the margin meant, but the menu itself seemed like a straightforward clue.

'Assuming he realises what date it is, I'm afraid he'll try

to carry out his original plan to stop the accident. But he won't want to scare Mum or me by just turning up. He's more likely to approach the past version of himself – his doppelganger – to warn him. The best place to find him alone would be the restaurant.'

She held up the menu.

'All right. The restaurant seems a good place to start. Can you take us there?'

'It's in Mount Major.'

'Ah. That's where I was stationed back then . . . or now I suppose.'

'Oh. Of course.' That's all they needed. More possible complications. What if David ran into *his* doppelganger in Mount Major? That was rule number two. Still, it was the best idea she had. They had to go there. They'd just have to be careful.

'We could catch the train back but it would be easier if we had a car.'

'Leave that to me.' She blinked and Rafael had disappeared.

'Where's he going?'

'I think he's gone to find us a car.'

They walked across the motel forecourt towards the road. After standing around for a few minutes, Rafael rumbled towards them in a blue Ford car. The paint was faded in places and there was some panel damage down the passenger side, but the engine sounded okay. David opened the front door and gestured for her to get into the passenger seat next to Rafael.

'Did you steal this car?'

He narrowed his eyes at her. 'Borrowed.'

She threw a glance at David as she slid in. He climbed into the back seat and Rafael put the car into gear.

They drove back down the main street and then turned left onto the highway. Feldham receded quickly as they passed by acres of farmland. She closed her eyes, remembering all the times she had travelled the same road in the back of her parents' car to the restaurant almost every weekend. Some kids might have been bored spending lots of nights in the kitchen of a family business, but she never minded. The restaurant always felt like a second home to her. The smell of garlic bread in the oven or pasta sauce on the stove was a comfort. And her father found ways to keep her occupied with puzzles or word games while her mother always brought plenty of books from the library.

As they approached a T-junction, she shivered and the skin on her scarred hand prickled. She sat up straight, tensed. Of course they would pass by this spot. How could she have forgotten?

'What's wrong?' David touched her shoulder.

'Slow down.' She undid her seatbelt but Rafael didn't respond.

'Stop!' she shouted.

He put the indicator on and eased the car onto the shoulder of the road beside a slightly bent out of shape street sign. The green and white letters on it spelled Ridgeway Lane, and there was an arrow pointing towards the turn-off.

Essie sat still for a long moment, trying to concentrate

on breathing. She hadn't been back. Not once in more than twenty years. After the accident, while she was still in the hospital recovering, her father had packed up everything and moved them to Mount Major. As she stared out the car window, she felt frozen, locked in a moment in time that, in some ways, had never ended.

Reality dissolved around her as the sensation of the car skidding and flipping over – once, twice – came back to her with a terrifying force. The rain speckled her face through the open roof as she was wedged in the back of the car, trapped by her seatbelt. Waiting. Frightened. Crying in the darkness. The thought hit her, like someone striking her face.

This is wrong. It's all wrong.

Maybe *she* had got it all wrong. What if the future Essie had made a mistake? What if this was the chance to make it all right? It was in her grasp. So close. All around her, the air seemed to pulsate with a strange energy, rippling and folding in on itself. She gripped her scarred hand and dug her nails into it, hoping the pain would break through and anchor her back in reality.

But it was David who broke into her consciousness.

'I remember. This is where it happened. The accident.'

He squeezed her shoulder gently. The energy surrounding her died down and slowly ebbed away, like receding waves on a shoreline. He had been there that night, too. The first officer on the scene.

Get hold of yourself, Essie.

She blinked and let out her breath. The scar on her hand was dappled with tiny, crescent shaped indents.

'I'm fine,' she said. 'Let's keep going.'

David's hand left her shoulder and Rafael eased the car back onto the road without any comment.

As they arrived on the outskirts of Mount Major, more memories came flooding back to her.

'That was my high school.' She pointed at the unappealing brown brick building. The iron gates were locked for the summer holidays and a sign out the front bore the school's insignia, a red and white shield with Mount Major Secondary School inscribed across it. Her stomach tensed thinking about the many awkward adolescence years she had spent there, mostly holed up in the school library – her own personal refuge. If the restaurant kitchen was her second home, the library was a close third. No one was allowed to talk in the library, so it didn't matter that she had hardly anyone to talk to anyway.

Further down the street, they passed her favourite ice cream shop. Her parents would sometimes take her there for a treat. She could almost taste the too-sweet flavours and the crisp, flaky cones. Rafael turned down a crossroad and a beautiful sandstone building came into view. Its slender spire reached heavenwards while arched windows framed the stone walls.

'My parents were married in that church,' she said, pointing. 'My grandma insisted on it, even though they weren't religious. Mum agreed because she didn't want to cause a fuss.'

Everywhere she looked there was some whisper of memory, and every memory was painfully divided between the time before and after the accident. No wonder her father had moved his restaurant to the city after she had gone away to university. No wonder she herself had stayed away so long.

'Head that way.' She pointed towards the central shopping area. *La Fortuna* was there, a small glass frontage facing the street. As the red and gold awning came into view, it seemed gaudier than she remembered it.

Rafael found a park just across the road from the shops and he locked up after they got out.

David fell into step next to Essie. 'The police station isn't far from here.'

She grimaced. She couldn't recall its exact location as she'd never been there. 'Let's try to avoid it. Remember Mum's rule about not meeting our doppelgangers?'

He nodded and they continued towards *La Fortuna*. The door was closed, inside dark. It was too early yet.

'We can wait in there.' She pointed to the *Little Pig Café* next door with its cartoon cutout piglet out the front. 'We should be able to see if Dad tries to come to the restaurant from there.'

Rafael had stopped walking, his grey eyes watchful.

'I keep lookout.' Peeling off, he vanished down an adjacent street without waiting for their agreement. David shook his head briefly and then led her into the café. They chose a table by the window where they would see anyone coming and going from the restaurant. A waitress with short grey hair handed them menus. Her stomach rumbled as she inhaled the smell of cooked food. It had been a while since she had anything to eat. She felt self-conscious ordering tea, eggs, bacon, mushrooms, and toast in front of David, but he insisted she eat well and she was starving. He only ordered a black coffee for himself and sat across from her, sipping it slowly, as she dug into her breakfast.

'What time would your father usually arrive at the restaurant?'

She shoved a mushroom in her mouth and chased it down with a sip of tea. 'I guess he would probably go in around ten or eleven to start preparing. He was only open for dinner.'

David flipped open his pocket watch.

'We still have about an hour to wait.' His eyes darted to the sidewalk, and she turned to see a young woman pushing a plump baby in a stroller. The woman stopped to glance at the menu posted in the window of *La Fortuna* before turning and walking on.

Essie licked her lips as she finished the last forkful of her food. She could feel David watching her again, and she met his gaze. His eyes were the nice green colour, the one she liked best, but his skin looked a little pale. He had seemed a bit unwell at the train station too. It occurred to her that maybe he was hungry, just not for human food.

'I know you're not eating anything on the menu. But are you *thirsty*?' His eyes remained on her, and he smiled calmly as he leaned in.

'You mean when did I last feed?' he stage-whispered.

Was he making fun of her? She fiddled with her teacup and arched her eyebrows at him. It was a legitimate question. If he suddenly keeled over from lack of sustenance, it wouldn't be helpful.

'I'm only asking because I thought with everything going on, you might have forgotten. And you look a little pale.'

'Am I?'

'If you needed *something*, I could probably help.' She stuck out her wrist and nodded towards it.

He didn't look down. His eyes never left hers. He simply shook his head resolutely.

'No, that's not a good idea.'

She pulled her wrist back. The whole idea of blood drinking was vile, but his outright rejection of her offer stung.

'Why not? It's the same as the blood bank, isn't it? We'd just be cutting out the middleman, or woman.'

'It's not the same.' His tone was clipped.

'Why?'

'Because I wouldn't trust myself with you. Or anyone who still has a heartbeat.'

She frowned. 'But you told me that the need for blood doesn't control you, not like the Bloodborns.'

He sat back, straightening in his chair.

'It doesn't control me. But that's partly due to physiology and partly because I choose not to indulge it. The potential is still there. I can feel it. There are some doors that should remain closed, even if one is reasonably confident of what they will find on the other side.' Essie stared down at her tea. For some reason, it felt like he was scolding her.

'I was only trying to help,' she murmured.

'I know.' His voice was gentler. He leaned across the

table and took her hand, squeezing it lightly. 'And I appreciate your thoughtfulness.' She smelt his scent of worn leather. His eyes darkened, and he leaned back.

'Anyway, I'm probably a bit pale because I had a headache earlier. Rafael and I took care of the blood situation before we left. He brought some supplies to your house when he came over.'

'The duffle bag.'

He nodded. 'We should be okay on that score for a few more days, barring any accident or injury.'

The scientist in her longed to know exactly what he meant. She had been maintaining a mental list of questions since she discovered his true nature. How long could they endure lack of blood? What effect did it have on their metabolism? But she sensed from his tone that he wouldn't elaborate any further right now. She sipped the rest of her tea, restraining her curiosity. He ordered another black coffee, and the morning wore on. Other diners came and left the café. By quarter past eleven, their plates had been cleared and there was still no sign of her father. She tapped her leg against her chair and fiddled with her napkin.

'I think we will need to order something else or move on.' David motioned with his head towards the grey-haired waitress who had circled their table.

Essie adjusted her glasses and strained to look out the window again. 'I don't understand. He should be here. Well, at least one version of him should be here.'

David leapt to his feet, rattling the table. His chair fell over backwards.

'Stay here.' He dashed out of the café. Her eyes followed him, but he quickly disappeared between a group of people on the sidewalk. She wiped her mouth with her napkin and stood up to follow him. The grey-haired waitress blocked her path.

'Would you like the bill now, love?'

Flipping over a page on her order pad, she tore out the docket for their table with a practiced air. 'Pay at the front,' she said, handing it over.

Essie took the docket impatiently and moved towards the front of the café. Her stomach clenched as she patted her pockets in the vain hope she might have even a few dollars on her. The man standing behind the register looked at her.

'My friend has money. He just had to step out, but he'll be back in a minute.'

The man lifted his chin slightly in acquiescence. She moved out of the way so he could serve another customer.

Twenty minutes later, when David still had not returned, the man, who she discovered was named Vern, told her she had to settle the bill or he would call the police.

'Are you short of money? Is that the issue?'

'I already told you, my friend has money. I'm sure he'll be back soon.'

'Love, I think your boyfriend's done a runner on you.' Vern pursed his lips.

'He's not my boyfriend,' she mumbled, trying not to betray her frustration, but Vern was unmoved.

'Can I do some dishes, or work off the debt some other way?'

He lifted his dark, bushy eyebrows at her and picked up the telephone. 'That kind of thing might work in the movies, but not in real life. I already have a good dishwasher.' He thumbed over his shoulder to an industrial looking machine.

She strained to see out the café window. Where could he be? Why would he abandon her like this?

'Yeah, hi, it's Vern from the *Little Pig*. I've got a lady here who tried to do a runner on the bill.'

Vern made her sit in a chair at the back of the café to wait for the police. The grey-haired waitress watched her closely until two uniformed officers arrived. Though she had recently opened a time travelling wormhole that had destroyed part of an old church, she was otherwise a law-abiding citizen. She had never tried to skip out on a bill or committed any other kind of theft in her life. And the timing could not have been worse. Vern spoke to the police briefly and pointed in her direction. What on earth had happened to David? And how was she going to explain her way out of this mess?

Chapter 7

David

When he left Essie at the café table, he was certain he had glimpsed Gilbert crossing the carpark outside. Pushing gently through a small throng of people, he emerged on the other side, but Gilbert was not there. Spinning around, he strode back to *La Fortuna* and tried the door handle, but it was still locked, the restaurant dark inside. Sighing, he turned to go back into the café when his nose quivered, picking up an unexpected scent. Not living, but not dead. Not human and not Bloodborn. A bit like Raf, but not exactly the same. His breath caught in his throat.

Eyes darting about, he tried to catch sight of the source. Seeing nothing out of place, he followed the scent to where it grew stronger, around the outside of the shopping centre complex and down an alley that led to an uncovered courtyard. A sour smell came from the garbage bags piled-up in the bins at the back of the shop fronts, but he could still make out the unfamiliar scent. It had to be the other Amaranthine. But where were they? He pivoted around in confusion, his eyes combing the various doorways. There was a stairwell leading to a second-floor balcony. He gazed up, but still, he saw nothing.

Had the headache the night before dulled his senses? Maybe he could not trust what he was smelling and seeing?

'Hello?' he shouted, turning in a full circle. A snigger echoed around him, and he pivoted in the direction from which it came. Glimpsing a movement on the balcony above, he squinted – it was the tell-tale blur of a creature moving too quickly to be human or even animal. A sense of unease slid over him.

He spun around again. 'Show yourself!'

A man in black jeans and a black T-shirt slipped from a doorway at the top of the stairs and into the light. His brown skin glowed in the sun, his eyes dark and wide. He blew a ring of smoke from his mouth and his lips curled. Flicking his cigarette butt to the ground, he vaulted over the balcony railing, several feet above, and landed gracefully in the courtyard. David glanced about, nervous that someone else might have seen him, but they looked to be alone.

'Astari!' The man's intense eyes remained fixed on David. Another figure appeared at the top of the stairs: a slender woman with long, dark hair. She was wearing a white lace jacket that grazed her ankles and contrasted beautifully with her honeyed skin.

He cleared his throat. 'I'm David Sorrow.'

The man did not respond right away, instead putting

his cigarettes in his back pocket nonchalantly before running a hand through his hair.

'I'm Dharma,' he said, finally. 'This is Astari.'

The woman tilted her head in acknowledgement and descended the remaining stairs to Dharma's side, her sheer jacket and long hair swishing gracefully as she moved.

'Where's your companion?' Dharma glanced over his shoulder, searching.

David frowned, thrown by the obvious knowledge sitting behind the question.

'I am not entirely sure.' He turned his head to follow Dharma's gaze, scanning for his friend. 'He was supposed to be playing lookout.'

'Well, he's not very good at it. How long has he been reverting?'

David grimaced again, his jaw tightening. How did this man know so much about Raf? Had they been following them, watching them?

'About one hundred years,' he answered absently, still feeling off balance.

Dharma made a loud whistling sound through his front teeth.

'Obviously losing his touch. But he still has a little while to go.' Resentment flared in David's chest and he narrowed his eyes at the young vampire.

A sudden rush of wind blew through the courtyard and Dharma whirled in response. Raf appeared beside David, holding Dharma's cigarette pack in his open palm.

'Not lost my touch, at least not yet.' Raf offered the

packet to Dharma. He took it sheepishly and Astari cut him a sideways glance.

'My apologies.' He gave Raf an exaggerated bow. 'I didn't mean to offend you.'

Raf spread his hands expansively. 'I am glad we see you. I sensed your presence at train station last night. It has been many decades since we meet others of our kind.'

Raf was quick to get to the point, but he also seemed careful not to give specifics. For instance, he hadn't mentioned that 'decades' included future ones yet to come. Dharma looked towards Astari, a question in his eyes. Clearly, she was in charge. She must be the elder of the two. She gave him a slight nod in response.

'We also have not seen others of our kind for a long time. Well, Astari hasn't. She only turned me a few years ago. We have been travelling around Asia hunting Bloodborns and came down here through Indonesia.'

David frowned, his detective instincts kicking in. 'Why here of all places? It's a bit out of the way.'

Dharma looked to Astari again, and again she nodded.

'We were drawn here. Astari has had strange dreams. We do not know what they mean yet, but she knew we had to come.'

A chill settled in his bones, and he exchanged a quick glance with Raf.

'You also have had the dreams.'

Astari's voice startled him. She locked her gaze with his for a long moment. Her dark eyes, framed with long, black lashes, changed to a deep bronze colour. As she stared at him, the visions from his dreams flashed through his mind.

What did she know of those scenes? The piles of Amaranthine bodies, their blood curdled in pools on the ground? Did she know the feeling of absolute dread they brought, as if nothing could ever overcome it? Her eyes bored into him. After a moment, he had to look away.

'How do you know about dreams?' Raf's expression was open, but his question had a cautious edge to it.

'Because I saw *you* in my dreams,' Astari replied. A tremor swept through his body, and he steeled himself against its effects.

'I saw both of you. And the human. The woman with the scarred hand who was with you in the café.'

The woman.

Essie.

David's mind snapped back to the table where he had abandoned her.

'Damn. I left Essie at the café, Raf. I need to get back to her.'

As he turned to leave, Dharma caught his arm.

'No point, Sorrow. She's not there anymore. The police marched her off a few minutes ago. I overheard them say something about her not paying the bill.'

'*Mio Dio.*' Raf's face was lined with frustration. 'Sometimes I think that woman is – how you say it – a magnet for trouble.'

His hands tensed into fists. This was all his fault for leaving her alone. And they would be taking her to the police station. Had he been on a shift today? What if Essie ran into him, the other version of him? Or what if something else happened to her? He had to get her out of police custody and quickly.

Dharma lit up another cigarette, puffing smoke into the air and dropping ash on the ground. Another flare of annoyance spread through David's chest.

'It's not Essie's fault. They will probably just take her to the station and give her a warning. But she won't be able to provide any identification which will raise suspicion. We need to get her out.'

He paced a few steps back and forth.

'But, I cannot go after her myself because I might see . . . well *me*. You probably should not go for that matter either, Raf.' Raf had been to the police station on occasion over the years. Someone could recognise him.

Both Dharma and Astari's eyes were on him. What he was saying would make absolutely no sense to them. But he didn't care. His priority was to get Essie back.

'So, the human woman is in trouble with human authorities?' Dharma blew a perfect ring of smoke. 'Not sure why that involves us.'

'Her name is Essie.' He gritted his teeth. 'Doctor Essie Thornton.'

'Ah, she's a doctor?'

'Yes. And neither Raf or I can go and get her. It's a long story. And you probably won't believe half of it anyway.'

'Try me.'

David tapped his hand against his thigh impatiently. How could he summarise their current situation without giving away too much detail? Was it even a wise idea, when Dharma seemed so casually indifferent? He took a breath.

'The three of us, Rafael, Essie and me, we're time travellers from the near future. Right now, there are two versions of me present in this town – me from the present timeline, and, well, me.' He pointed at himself. 'The me from this timeline could be in that police station right now. And the two of us should never meet.'

Dharma pressed his lips together, but his eyes glinted as his body shook with laughter. He stopped when he noticed Raf's stern expression.

Astari only nodded, seeming completely unfazed.

'That somehow makes sense,' she said serenely, as if it was the sort of thing she heard every day. Dharma opened his mouth, but a look from Astari silenced him again. Something flashed in her eyes.

'We can help you get Doctor Essie back.' As she smiled, she flashed a row of white, straight teeth and rested her hand on Dharma's shoulder. 'I would very much like to meet her and hear more about this time travel. In all my long years, there is something new at last. It sounds fascinating.'

'It is settled then,' Raf said, crossing his arms over his chest. 'Our new friends will retrieve the *dottore* from the police.'

David hesitated. He was not sure yet that he would call them friends. Especially Dharma. But they could certainly use the help, and he wasn't sure how else he could get Essie out of trouble.

'Fine.'

Dharma sent one last puff of smoke into the air before dropping the cigarette butt on the ground. Astari sent him a meaningful look.

'Okay, *I'll* go rescue your girl for you I guess.'

David pulled his shoulders back and pressed his lips together. So many things about that sentence grated on him, but he swallowed his frustration.

Essie. We need to get to Essie.

'Since I used to work there, I can give you some pointers on getting in and out undetected.'

'If it makes you feel better, but I doubt I'll need any help.'

Astari clipped Dharma lightly over the ears. David would have liked to hit him quite a bit harder, but he didn't want to cause any further delays by starting a fight. They had to get to Essie and make sure she was safe.

'I know a back way to the police station,' he sighed. 'Let's go.'

Chapter 8

Essie

Essie tried to sit still, but the chair had a hard back and no seat padding. The officer across from her tapped his pen on the interview room desk impatiently. She couldn't remember his first name because she was too nervous when he introduced himself in the café. Lucas or Luke. Something like that. His surname was definitely Barnes though, because that was printed on the badge pinned to his uniform, under his title of Senior Constable. Her eyes drifted to the clock on the wall above his head and she watched the second hand tick by. It was now getting on towards mid-afternoon. She had no idea where her father was, or David for that matter, and it seemed like she might be getting arrested. Or at least held for questioning.

'I'm sorry, Ms Smith. Am I keeping you from something important?' Barnes kept tapping the pen.

Her gaze snapped back to him, and she forced a smile as she shook her head. She had given him a fake name, of course, but lying didn't come easily to her and she had faltered trying to come up with a bogus address, so she defaulted to saying she was staying at a friend's and couldn't remember it. A fluorescent light buzzed overhead as the silence dragged on. At last Barnes spoke again.

'You probably think skipping out on a bill isn't a big deal. What's a few free meals? Well, here in Mount Major, those free meals are people's livelihoods. And we've had a spate of this lately.'

'I really am sorry,' she said. 'I fully intended to pay, but as I told you at the café, my friend ran out on me, and he had our money.' She didn't need to lie about that part. David had run out on her.

'Well, your "friend", isn't much of a friend if he just walked out on you.'

No kidding.

Even though she was annoyed at him, she was also worried that something could have happened. He would not have abandoned her without a good reason. She was sure of it.

'Paulson has had a look, and you aren't in any police records.'

She smiled and kept quiet, the insistent tapping of Barnes' pen as maddening as a dripping tap. When he looked down at his paperwork, she stole a glance around the room, registering a window on the wall to her left. There was a knock on the interview room door, and Barnes looked up. She turned her face back to him and fixed her smile in place again as the door clicked open.

'Ah, Sorrow,' Barnes said with a slight wave of his

hand. Her smile slipped and her body froze. Did he say Sorrow? She must have misheard him.

'Good afternoon, Senior Constable. I am sorry to interrupt. I have just reported for my shift. The Sergeant said you had the roster.'

She didn't need to turn around and check, because there was absolutely no doubt. She would know the formal cadence of that voice anywhere. So much for the rule about staying away from their doppelgangers.

'Yes. I put you on cleaning down the lock-up today.'

'As in the cells, downstairs, where we lock people up?' David asked. Essie caught Barnes suppressing a grin before he replied.

'That's right. The drunks, the parole offenders, people who skip out on bills.'

Barnes threw a glare in her direction. Her heart was beating so fast that blood rushed to her head.

Please let him leave. Please let him leave.

'Right then,' David replied. She heard the door click shut and released a slow breath.

Barnes turned his attention back to her. 'New guy, hasn't been around long.'

Essie nodded in a stilted way, registering the irony of Barnes' comment.

If only he knew how long that guy has been around.

'Hmm, what to do with you?' he pondered, the tapping starting up again. 'We don't generally arrest first-time offenders for this type of thing. But it's not like you're a teenage hooligan who should have known better. And it's difficult to verify your identity without at least a street address.' He raised his eyebrows at her as if giving her one last chance to provide it. When she kept silent, he stood up.

'Wait here while I go and talk to the Sergeant.'

As soon as Barnes had closed the door behind him, she leapt to the window. Even if she stood on a chair, it was mounted too high on the wall for her to see out properly, let alone try to escape through it.

Crap, crap, crap.

What would Barnes do with her? Surely, they didn't put people in the lock-up for bilking on a café breakfast. That was just a joke, right? On the other hand, it didn't sound like he would let her go. Not without confirming where she was staying.

The air stirred and cigarette smoke filled her nostrils. She started, stepping backwards as a dark-haired man in black appeared in front of her.

'Don't scream,' he said, holding his hands up in a calming motion. 'I'm Dharma. Your boyfriend sent me. David Sorrow.'

David?

She stared at him, trying to comprehend what was happening. His eye colour lightened from almost pitch black to a burnt orange.

His eyes changed colour.

Her hand came to rest on her stomach as fear and excitement gripped her in equal measure. Changing eye colour had been one of her first clues to David's real identity. Before he had shared his secret with her. It was a hallmark of the Amaranthine. So, this man had to be

Amaranthine too. He had to be the one who Rafael had sensed.

'He's not my boyfriend.' She shook her head, embarrassed. That had to be the least relevant thing to mention at that moment.

'Whatever.'

Dharma glanced over his shoulder. She pushed her glasses up her nose, taking in the detail of him. He was tall. Not as tall as David, maybe just under six feet. But he looked younger than David. Really young. Maybe in his early twenties.

'Where is David? Is he okay?'

'He's fine,' he said, waving his hand. 'He said he had to wait outside – some crazy story about time travel and meeting himself. Anyway, let's go.'

He extended his hand to her. She studied it. He might be Amaranthine, but he was still a complete stranger. He had mentioned time travel though, and only David or Rafael could have told him about that. They must have sent him, or at least have met him. She glanced up at the high window on the wall. There weren't really any other options if she wanted to get out of the police station. And she had to escape before Barnes decided to put her in the lock-up where the other David Sorrow was probably cleaning toilets right now.

'Okay. What's your plan?'

'Easy,' he replied, offering her his hand again. His whole demeanour seemed to match that one word. *Easy.* He eyed her up and down. 'You're pretty small. We can sneak out of here too fast for anyone to see. The only catch is it might make you feel a bit sick.'

'Sick?' she echoed. But before she had a chance to ask any more questions, he grabbed her hand and encircled her waist with his other arm. Air rushed against her skin. She barely had time to register the haze of faces as they passed through the station and out the door before they abruptly halted and he dropped her on the ground. She doubled over, trying to catch her breath. Her throat burned, the contents of her stomach rising in her chest. She swallowed hard, trying to hold down her breakfast.

'Are you all right?' David was gently rubbing circles on her back. She coughed and he pressed his handkerchief into her hand. Not for the first time was she grateful that he had the habit of always carrying a handkerchief. She seemed to use them a lot more than he did. Wiping her wet lips, she straightened up.

'Was that really necessary?' David glared at Dharma.

'You told me to get her out of there.'

Dharma winked at her. Despite the nausea-inducing speed of the trip, she had to admit it was kind of thrilling.

'Relax. You'll feel better in a minute.' He took a pack of cigarettes from his pocket and lit up. David looked like he was about to say something to him when Rafael stepped forward with a woman at his side. The woman's dark hair fell in thick, waist-length waves. Her face was achingly symmetrical. She had high set cheekbones and a pair of large, almond-shaped eyes that transformed into a caramel colour as she held Essie's gaze.

'You're . . . you're one of them, aren't you?' she stammered.

The woman nodded, a smile playing on her full, red-pink lips.

'This is Astari,' Dharma said, moving to stand beside the woman.

Astari.

Essie repeated the name in her head. It was a beautiful name that matched the woman's ethereal beauty.

'She's the elder of us, and *I* am the younger. Younger, hotter, and more fun.' He shot Essie a grin and another wink.

She found herself smiling. Something about his impishness was refreshing, even if he had nearly caused her to vomit her breakfast.

So, these were the other Amaranthine. The four of them together raised goosebumps on the back of her neck.

Standing side by side with the other Amaranthine, the attributes that she had overlooked when she had first met David – his eyes changing colour, his suppressed strength, his otherworldliness – were much harder to dismiss. He had told her that being restricted to hereditary pairs was a population control mechanism – it prevented a proliferation of Amaranthine, a failsafe against them becoming like the Bloodborns. But maybe it was also that living in isolated pairs acted as an evolutionary defence against discovery by humans. There were so many new questions about vampire biology to add to her mental list.

Suddenly David grimaced and clutched the side of his head, leaning forwards.

'What is it?'

'The headache again,' he stammered. 'It's worse though. It feels like someone is stabbing a knife into my brain.'

Essie frowned. 'I saw you – the other you – in the police station. Or, rather, I heard him. He didn't see me. The headaches could be from the two versions of you being too close together. Maybe that's one of the reasons we were warned to avoid them – our doppelgangers.' She tried to put her arm around his shoulders to steady him, but he was too tall. Astari stepped in to help, taking his other elbow.

Essie glanced back nervously at the police station, envisaging Constable David Sorrow emerging from the front door at any moment.

'Did police mention recent murders, missing peoples?' Rafael asked, seemingly unconcerned about David's worsening condition.

'Not that I heard,' she responded impatiently. David groaned again and keeled to the side. 'We need to get him away from here, somewhere he can recover, and we can regroup.' She leaned in, trying to offer him more support.

'We know a place,' Astari said. 'It's not far away.'

'I'll be all right,' David protested, trying to straighten up. 'We need to find your father.' He tried to take a step forwards, but doubled over again, gripping his head.

Essie bit down on her front lip, anxiety creeping up.

'Take us there, please,' she said to Astari, without waiting for either Rafael or David to agree.

Chapter 9

David

'Stop here.' Dharma pointed.

David raised his head carefully to look out the window. Rafael pulled the stolen car up against the curb where Dharma had indicated and turned off the engine. It was a nondescript suburban street full of average houses. The lawns were mostly trimmed, and the gardens were well kept. The heat of mid-afternoon was slowly fading, and a cool breeze wafted over his face as he got out of the car. It felt sweet against his clammy skin. The pressure in his head was slowly fading. But his legs moved like lead and just as he felt he might stumble, Essie was at his elbow, steadying him.

'I've got you,' she said softly. He sighed at the complete reversal of roles. He was used to being physically superior – faster, stronger, more durable. He was used to being the protector, not the one who needed help at every turn.

Back at the shopping centre, Astari had separated from

the group to find some human food. Essie had almost lost most of the only meal she'd had recently in the carpark, thanks to Dharma's carelessness. At least Astari seemed more attentive about such things.

'This way,' Dharma beckoned with a crooked finger. They followed him down a narrow path that ran between the rear of the houses. He stopped outside a white, rusted gate. It squeaked open as he gently nudged it with his hip.

'We've been using this as a base. It's empty.' He headed up a small set of stairs that opened onto a wide, enclosed porch which stretched the length of the back of a weatherboard house. The tinkle of a wind chime sounded as he bumped his head on it.

'How do you know it's empty?' Essie asked, looking about furtively, her voice edged with uncertainty.

'It's okay, Doc, we've been staying here since we arrived. The owners are on holidays in Queensland for a few weeks, according to Lorraine.'

'Lorraine?'

Dharma thumbed in the direction of the house next door. The back garden was full of colourful pots of woody geraniums and a giant, wilted hydrangea.

'Neighbour. I heard her telling her son while she was out watering.'

Dharma reached for the handle on the sliding glass door. David's hand shot out to stop him.

'You didn't mention we'd be breaking and entering.'

Dharma had managed to get his hackles up again. The younger vampire pushed open the door with ease.

'I didn't break anything when I entered.' He smirked, winking at Essie again as he slid through the door. She grinned back and David scowled. This was exactly how trouble started with humans – getting caught for small misdemeanours. But he was too exhausted to fight about it. Raf took his other arm, and he leaned on both him and Essie to drag his feet inside.

They entered a small lounge room with an adjoining kitchen. At the other end of the kitchen, a hallway led towards the front of the house. The lounge room was furnished with a floral settee, two armchairs, and a modest-sized television. The dainty furnishings suggested the owners were an older couple. Raf and Essie lowered him into one of the chairs and he leaned his head back against it as he closed his eyes. He wasn't sure how long he sat like that, until, at some point, he started to feel normal again. Essie pressed her hand to his forehead and he relished her cool touch.

'Feeling better?' He could hear the anxiety in her voice. He didn't want her to be worried about him.

'Yes.' The pain had subsided. He exhaled and opened his eyes.

'You do not need hover over him like that,' Raf said from across the room. 'He will be fine.'

'And how do you know that?' she snapped, snatching her hand away. 'Because the Amaranthine don't get sick? Well, he is sick, and we don't even know what's wrong with him!'

Raf made a scoffing noise and David raised his hands to

quiet their argument. Essie stepped back a little and then blinked rapidly as a rush of movement whooshed around them. Astari appeared in the kitchen, upending a shopping bag on the bench. A random assortment of groceries fell out of it. A bottle of milk, a couple of apples, a loaf of bread and some peanut butter.

'I hope there's something you like here, Doctor Essie. It's been a while since I bought food for a human.'

Essie crossed to the kitchen and reached for a mug. 'Thank you. I might make some tea.'

He followed Essie's movements in the kitchen. She filled the kettle with water and set it to boil. The vampires sat down on the floral settee. Dharma looked at him expectantly.

'Okay, I think we've earned the truth,' he said. 'What are you really doing here? Cause that whole time travel thing – that's a joke, right?'

David leaned forwards in his seat and rested his elbows on his knees, tenting his fingers. It was a fair question. As annoying as he found the young vampire to be, if he were in the same position, he would ask the same thing. Exchanging a quick glance with Raf, he noted the slight tilt of his head and took it as a sign he should be open with them.

'It is not a joke,' he said. 'We travelled here from twenty-five years in the future.' He paused, watching their reactions. Dharma still looked sceptical. Astari's face was inscrutable.

Essie set down a cup of tea in front of him. 'Here,' she

said. 'This might help your head. Or not. But try it.' He smiled appreciatively as he picked up the cup.

'We are telling the truth,' Essie said, taking a seat with them. She peeled back the cuff of her sleeve, revealing the Time Weaver that Rhonda had given her.

'This device allows us to travel in time. We came here to find my father. He fell through a wormhole. It's like a time travel tube. We have to find him and take him back with us to the future.'

Astari leaned forwards slightly, her eyes on the Time Weaver, while Dharma scratched his chin, his left knee bobbing up and down.

'Okay, say that's all true. Where's your dad now? Why don't you just grab him and go?'

'We don't know exactly where he is yet,' Essie responded. 'He might not even realise what has happened to him. He could be disoriented or lost.' She pushed her sleeve back down, covering the bracelet. 'But what we do know is that tomorrow night, my whole family is in a car accident not far from here, on Ridgeway Lane.' Her eyes glistened. 'My mother dies on the scene.'

His heart clenched. But her face hardened, and she went on. 'If my dad realises the timing, he'll try to stop the accident.'

'But wouldn't that be a good thing?' Dharma asked. 'Don't you want to save your mum?'

Essie hesitated, met his eyes, then glanced away.

David cleared his throat. 'It's not that simple, unfortunately. There are rules for time travel, rules that stop the whole fabric of time from tearing apart. One of them is that we can't change certain events like this. It could have unexpected consequences.'

Dharma whistled through his teeth, his knee still jiggling.

'Jeez. Surely, it's worth a shot though.'

Essie's lip trembled, and he tensed as his anger flared. Couldn't Dharma see how hard this was for her? Astari reached out and gently stilled Dharma's bouncing knee.

'I'm sorry, Doctor Essie. This must be a very difficult situation. I'm sure there are things that all of us would want to change in the past, if we could.'

Essie shrugged, her eyes dry again.

'I have to put aside my feelings about it and stick to the rules. I'm a temporal physics lecturer. I invented this technology – or I will,' she said, holding up her wrist again. 'I understand how complex it is – how everything is connected. So many things could go wrong if we ignore the rules, or if my father does. That's why we have to find him and take him back as soon as we can.'

There was a short silence, and David realised that mercifully, his headache had almost subsided entirely.

'Right,' Dharma said, still sounding somewhat unconvinced. 'If you're really from the future, tell us something about it. Is it like the movies? Are there flying cars and hover boards?'

A smile creased Essie's face, lighting her up.

'I'm sorry, but it's not like *Back to the Future*. I know it all sounds as crazy as a movie though.'

'It's not crazy.'

Dharma huffed. 'You don't actually believe all this, Astari?'

She threw him a dark look.

'How is it any more unbelievable than the reality of our existences? Doctor Essie says everything is connected, and I agree with her. I cannot help but feel like some force has drawn us all together.'

Raf shifted his posture, tilting his head.

'Two new Bloodborns fell through wormhole with old man. In our time, in future, we killed their maker, Sabine.'

'So you and David are here to hunt them also?'

Raf nodded at her. 'That is our vow. We exist to protect humanity from them.'

Dharma drew the packet of cigarettes and a lighter from his pocket.

'That, at least, is something I understand.' He tapped the end of a cigarette on the packet. 'We can help with the hunting. Not sure about the old man though.'

David exhaled. He wasn't sure how they would find Essie's father either. Rhonda's clue, the restaurant menu, hadn't panned out. But he was sure he didn't want Dharma's help with any of it.

'Thanks,' he said. 'But Rafael and I have hunted Bloodborns alone for over a century. We'll be fine.'

'Is that how long it's been since you saw other Amaranthine?' Astari crossed her legs elegantly.

Raf gave a short nod. 'At least. Have you met others, besides us?'

She shook her head slowly. 'No, not for as long as you.

But I have not really been looking. I've had this one to take care of and train for the past decade.'

Dharma screwed up his face at her. 'Here I thought it was me taking care of you.'

He placed the cigarette between his lips and went to light up.

'No,' David said, glaring at him. 'Breaking into this house is one thing, but you *can't* smoke in here.'

Dharma shrugged and let himself out the back door, closing the fly screen behind him. Raf and Astari sat talking a while longer while Essie ate a peanut butter sandwich and fussed over him, checking if he was feeling better. The two elders had many questions for each other. Astari's eyes flickered to him occasionally, but there was a palpable sense of comradery between her and Raf, their heads leaning close together. Astari's graceful movements and calm demeanour made him think she was old. At least as old as Rafael. He supposed there was an affinity between them that two such immortal beings could only know in each other's company. He was happy for his friend, while a part of him also grieved the same inevitable future he would face in the end. Astari and Dharma had not met others either. If the four of them were the last of the Amaranthine, he may eventually become one of a kind. Peerless.

Outside, the blue summer sky had begun to fade to dusky pink. Soon it would be night. The breeze through the fly screen picked up, dropping the temperature. He slid the door closed as Essie wrapped her arms around her shoulders, trying to stifle a yawn.

'Come on,' he said, stretching out his hand to her. 'It's been a long day. There must be an empty bed in this house where you can rest.'

She frowned back at him. 'But now that you're better, I thought we'd try to find my dad. Time is running out, David.'

'If you don't take some rest, you won't be any help. We will try again tomorrow.'

She took his hand reluctantly and allowed him to pull her to her feet. They left the others behind in the lounge room as he led her down the hallway.

'It's annoying being the only human here,' she mumbled, trailing behind him. 'Always the one needing food and rest.'

He stopped outside a room with a plump looking double bed covered in a patterned duvet.

He turned to her and smiled. 'I've had a few *human* moments today, too.' He touched the side of his head carefully.

Her eyebrows drew together in a frown.

'Are you really feeling better?' She reached up to press the back of her hand to his skin. He tried to steady the reaction of his heartbeat to her touch, conscious that though she could not hear it, the others surely would.

'Yes,' he said softly.

She hummed her satisfaction with his answer and flicked on the bedroom light. Walking over to the end of the bed, she sank down.

'David,' she said, as she unzipped her boots and toed them off. 'What will we do if we can't find him?' He could hear the strain in her voice. He crossed his arms over his chest as he leaned his shoulder against the doorframe.

'We will.' He tried to sound upbeat, reassuring.

'But he wasn't at the restaurant. After what happened with Sabine and Steenberger, maybe I really don't know him like I thought I did, so I can't predict what he'll do. Or what if he got lost or confused or hurt? And now we don't have long until...'

He thought for a moment before inclining his head.

'The future version of you sent us here to find him, so she must already have known the outcome. She had lived it before. We have to trust that she knew what she was doing.'

Her hands fidgeted in her lap. 'But what if we already changed something just by being here, and now the past that she remembered has changed because of it, and there's a giant ripple effect, and my mother...'

She squeezed her eyes closed and hugged her arms around her shoulders.

She was trying to hold the pieces of herself together – the part of her that knew what made sense, knew what road she should follow. And the other part, the part that longed for something else, something that seemed equally as important, even if it made no sense. He knew because he knew how she felt. His own emotions warred inside him, in mirror to hers, the unending struggle of push and pull he always felt in her presence. He wanted to comfort her, to be near her. He imagined taking her in his arms, holding her, his hands in her hair. The depth of his desire was strong and growing the more time he spent with her, like a force he'd never known before. But Raf's words echoed in his ears as well.

She is mortal.

There was no way to deny that they were from different worlds. Her life was so fleeting compared to his. One day, he would be like Raf. Surely it would be easier to make the journey into eternity alone, without any ties binding him to the things that are finite. At best, being part of his world would take Essie away from the human one and all the experiences she was destined to have. At worst, she would encounter trouble and danger with him, as she already had. There were threats he might not be able to protect her from, himself included.

And yet, he also could not deny there was a part of him that was still human. And that part longed for human things. Longed for her. With a deep sigh, he gave up the battle to keep his distance and crossed the room. Sinking down beside her, he stretched his arm around her shoulder. She leaned towards him and buried her face into his chest.

'Everything will be all right.' He stroked her hair.

She sniffed. 'But we don't know that.'

'No, but I do know you. Whatever plan you had, you would have considered it from all the angles. You know everything there is to know about this subject. I have faith in you. Even if you don't have faith in yourself.' She drew back and looked up at him, her expression guarded but hopeful.

'And we aren't taking our cues from the movies. We're driving a stolen Ford, not a stolen 1988 Delorian.'

She laughed. 'You've seen *Back to the Future*?'

He smiled. 'I may have been born in the late nineteenth century but I've tried to keep up with cinema over the years.'

Her lip quirked. 'You don't like Dharma much, do you?'

The question surprised him. He tipped his head, trying to temper his response.

'He is a bit reckless for my taste. I find it hard to abide.'

'Because you're so old and wise?' She grinned up at him, her eyes glinting. He chuckled.

'Something like that.'

The sound of the television came through the walls. It was the late news headlines. He instinctively reached for his mobile phone to check the internet. No use. It wasn't there. He could also hear whispers, voices Essie would not detect. Dharma was urging them to go out again, to look for Gilbert and the Bloodborns. Get it over with. They discussed weapons. Dharma said he had a small blade. He sighed. It was probably a good idea for them to go, even if it came from the boy. But all of that could happen while Essie slept. With any luck, they might even make some headway before morning.

'Time for some sleep.' He stood up, gesturing for her to lie down.

'Okay.' She yawned again, taking off her glasses and placing them on the nightstand. She crawled under the duvet and curled onto her side. 'Promise me you'll wake me if anything happens.'

'I promise,' he said as he crossed the room and turned off the light.

'David,' she whispered urgently. He stopped in the doorway, his hand resting on the frame.

Two of her heartbeats passed and then she took a breath.

'Thank you for coming with me. I'm glad you're here.'

He smiled into the darkness.

'Goodnight,' he whispered before slipping away.

Chapter 10

David

Astari was alone in the lounge room, standing at the back door. She turned slowly when he entered, her eyes watchful.

'How is Doctor Essie?'

'Sleeping, hopefully.'

He sat down on the settee and ran his fingers through his hair, massaging his head.

'Feeling better?'

He nodded. At least it didn't feel like his skull was being crushed any more.

'You didn't want to join the hunting party?'

She smiled at him knowingly. 'I'm sure they can handle it. And I wanted to speak to you alone. Will you tell me about your dreams, David?'

He shivered involuntarily. The image came to him again, like a photograph. So many bodies, one piled on top of the other. And so much red. As if a great river of blood had spilled its banks and bathed them in it. And then the end. The worst part. He squeezed his eyes shut against the memory.

'I keep seeing bodies. Many of our kind slaughtered, some dismembered. And each time, a figure in a dark hood stands over them, holding one of their severed heads in his hand. I can't make out his face.' He paused. 'But more awful than what I see, it's the feeling the dreams leave with me that's the worst. It's like a cold ache, deep in my bones. A dread that lingers long after I wake up.'

Astari sat down opposite him and rested her folded hands in her lap. For the first time since he'd met her, concern lined her features. At length she said, 'I have seen him too. This figure. And the slaughtered ones. What do you know of the Exile?'

The name triggered a memory in the back of his brain. He sifted through information, trying to recall the details.

'The Exile, as in Enki? As in ...'

Astari nodded. 'The father of all Bloodborns. The one who made them.'

'Raf told me of the legend – bits and pieces over the decades we've been together. He was supposedly a god, and he created the Bloodborns using his own immortal blood. He wanted an army to do his bidding, to help him secure dominion over the human race. But it went wrong. The Bloodborns he created were too animalistic, unpredictable.'

She raised one perfectly arched eyebrow at him. 'He also managed to enslave a small group of humans, but he underestimated their cunning.' She paused, her eyes glinting as if she were remembering an important detail. 'They worked in secret to find a way to create half-vampires, men and women with the strength and speed of the Bloodborns, but not ruled by blood lust. The original Amaranthine. With their help, the humans overthrew him, killing him and his closest disciples.'

David shrugged. 'I must admit, I've never completely believed the story. But if Enki ever existed, he's long gone.'

'Mmm.'

She flicked her long hair out behind her and rested her head against the back of the settee.

'What's Enki got to do with our dreams?'

Her eyes narrowed. 'I believe he is the dark figure we have both seen.'

'But why would we be dreaming of him now if he's gone? Is it a dream of the past?'

She sat up again, her lips quirking at the corners.

'Or perhaps a vision of the future. What if Enki did not die, as the legend says? What if he has been alive all this time, and he will return? I have been Amaranthine almost three hundred years now, but the more I see, the more I realise I don't yet know.'

He sighed, cupping his stubbled chin. So she was old. But Raf was still older. And he had never come across Enki. 'I don't mean to doubt you, Astari, but if Enki survived, where has he been all this time? And why would he reappear now?'

As he spoke, the last part of the dream burst into his

mind, robbing the air from his lungs. He shuddered out a breath as a cold wave swept through his veins.

'What's wrong?'

He hesitated. He hadn't told Raf about it because he didn't think he would understand. But he also didn't want to speak the words aloud. It would make it seem too real. Maybe telling Astari would help. What if she had dreamed that part too?

'At the end of my dream, the figure in black and Essie are together. She looks beautiful. And after he's slaughtered all the Amaranthine, he takes her by the hand and leads her into darkness.'

She studied him quietly for a moment. He felt as exposed as he feared he would.

'You care for her, don't you?'

Slightly surprised by her change of topic, he paused, weighing his response.

'Raf always taught me not to get involved with humans. Our vow is to protect them, and the best way to do that is to remain apart.'

The muscles across her jaw tightened for an instant. Then her expression softened.

'Perhaps Rafael is wise. It's too late for you though, isn't it?'

He opened his mouth to deny her implication. The words refused to come.

'I have been with the two of you for less than a day, but I see the way your eyes follow her, your scent is all over her...'

He cleared his throat, adjusted his tie.

'Raf means well. He's worried about me.'

She leaned forwards in her seat, her hands resting in her lap.

'I have loved many humans over the centuries of my existence, David. Two husbands I have buried, many lovers I have left behind. The accumulated loss is sometimes unbearable, intolerable.'

A distance passed through her eyes, as if she were reliving something inside her head.

'Then why did you do it?'

He searched her face for answers. Her gaze eventually flitted back to him, back to the present moment. A sad smile curled the edges of her lips.

'I suppose I did it because the alternative was even more painful to bear – the thought of walking this earth for as long as we do and never knowing intimacy. We want another to know us, to see us as we truly are and to accept us anyway. We are slaves to it as much as the Bloodborns are enslaved to blood, without reason or restraint. It is the part of us that is still human. The part we cannot ever leave behind.'

He sank back into the couch, the truth of her words settling into his bones. Essie knowing his secret, knowing who he really was, was both terrifying and addictive for him. It was also the most real thing he had felt in over a century. The dessert that he now recognised as his own soul thirsted for it. She had woken something he realised he had feared was lost to him forever. She made him feel more human. And because of her, he knew he never wanted to leave that part of him behind even if he could.

But he didn't really know how she felt about him. Even if she wanted to be in his life, was that a risk he should let her take? In the silence of the night, he attuned his ear to the thrum of her familiar human heart, only metres away from him. The rhythm was steady and peaceful.

Chapter 11

Essie

Dawn's first light seeped through the curtains. Essie bolted upright, trying to catch her breath, her heart sprinting. Disoriented and uncertain of her surroundings, the fragments of the dream she had woken from crashed into reality.

She was eight years old again, in the back of the family car. The passing streetlights cast a gentle glow and her eyes were heavy. She could hear her mother and father talking in the front seat, but not what they were saying. The scene went black. Then she was standing on the edge of the dark road. Ridgeway Lane. The family car was coming towards her, faster and faster. Her parents were in the front. She screamed to tell them to stop, but no sound came out. She tried to move, to wave her arms, but they hung at her sides like lumps of lead.

The car whooshed past, sweeping her hair back from her face. It swerved, flipped, and came to land on its side. Then her mother wasn't in the car anymore. She was standing beside her. She reached out, desperate to hold on to her. But her mother's figure faded, dissolving like vapour. She slipped through her fingers and was gone, leaving only a grinding ache in her heart. She tried to push down the loneliness, the crushing emptiness, but it grew inside her, bubbling up from her chest, overflowing.

She brushed away the tears on her cheeks with the back of her hand.

It was just a dream. Don't let this shake you.

David appeared in the doorway. 'Are you all right? I heard ...'

She put on her glasses, and he came into focus, leaning in the doorway. Heat rushed to her cheeks as she remembered how he had held her the night before while she cried. His chest was broad and muscled and he smelled so good. She didn't meet his eyes.

'I'm fine. Any luck finding Dad?'

He shook his head slowly.

'Come to the kitchen when you're ready. We'll catch you up.'

She used the bathroom to take a quick shower, trying not to make any mess. Even though she had to put her old clothes back on, it felt good to be clean underneath. In the lounge room, the vampires sat facing each other. Their quiet chatter stopped when she entered. Feeling self-consciously human, she grabbed an apple from the bench and bit into it as she sat down.

'So, what's the situation?' she asked as she chewed.

Dharma looked to Rafael, but from the older vampire's

blank stare, it seemed he was thinking about something else.

'We went out last night. But we didn't have any luck finding your dad, Doc.'

'I don't understand. There aren't *that* many places he could be.'

'We checked the hospital, parks, asked around. No one has seen anyone who looks like him.'

She took another bite of her apple and tossed the core onto the coffee table. Nothing was making any sense. Maybe she had missed something? They needed to go back to the start and review all the information her mother had given them again.

'Okay, let's assume he arrived here, but maybe he's confused. He doesn't know what's going on or that he's in the past. We know he won't try going home. And we know he hasn't tried the restaurant yet.'

She stood up and started pacing as she finished chewing the last bite of apple. She always did her best thinking when she was moving. In contrast, the vampires were preternaturally still, except Dharma, who was flipping a coin along his knuckles, catching it in his palm and starting again. He was so un-vampire-like, it made Essie grin despite herself.

'Can you think of somewhere else your father would go?' David asked.

She shrugged, feeling defeated.

'When I was a kid, I didn't pay that much attention to where Dad was when he wasn't with me.'

She shoved her fists into her pockets. Her hand closed

around the crumpled restaurant menu. She pulled it out and unfolded it again. It was the clue that led them to the restaurant. But the restaurant was a bust. Was there more to the menu? Did it mean something else?

She placed it on the coffee table where they could all see it and smoothed out the creases, running her eye over the dishes she knew so well. Pesto pasta. Meatballs. Lasagne. Typical Italian fare at reasonable prices. That would have been *La Fortuna*'s tagline, if it had one. When she read the name of the next dish, she stopped. fettucine Alfredo. She couldn't remember that one. Her eyes flicked to the price. It was far more expensive than any of the other dishes. She stared more closely, examining the rest of the menu. Pizzas, salad. It was all there. Except there was one dish that was missing. The risotto. Her Dad's famous risotto. He called it Risotto a la Gilbert II after the famous French actor, who had apparently invented risotto in the first place. She smiled to herself as she remembered how he would often pluck a piece of spaghetti and put it on his top lip as he pranced about the kitchen pretending to be French with his spaghetti moustache. Why was there Fettucine Alfredo on this version of the menu, but no risotto? She flipped it over and back again.

As she stared at the dishes and prices, the letters and numbers began to move and re-assemble in her mind.

'Oh,' she breathed.

What's wrong?' David asked.

She pushed her glasses up, frowning.

'I made a mistake. This menu is a clue, but it's more complicated than I thought.'

'What do you mean?' Dharma palmed his coin and leaned forwards.

'It's a cipher,' she said. 'Dad used to give me these types of puzzles to keep me occupied when I had to stay with him at the restaurant. I need a pen.'

David handed her one. She uncapped it and began scrawling on the paper. Ink smudged across the page as she jotted down letters and then crossed them out, analysing the frequency of the characters in the cipher. It looked like there should be a keyword. She started experimenting with possibilities, arranging and rearranging combinations. A shadow appeared over her shoulder.

'Ah, I know this,' Rafael said. 'These were used in the war.'

She hummed an acknowledgement and turned back to her work, trying out more keywords. Menu, restaurant, dining. Nothing seemed to fit. Tapping the pen on the table, she looked over the menu again. The curious phrase pencilled in the margin jumped out at her.

The absence will reveal the presence.

Could that be it? She looked down at the menu again and mentally re-arranged more letters.

'I've got it,' she exclaimed, scrawling the word on the page. 'The key is RISOTTO. It's the dish that was on the menu and isn't there anymore. It's been replaced with fettucine Alfredo instead.'

David frowned and Dharma and Rafael hovered over her as she worked quickly, letter by letter, shifting each word in the description of fettucine Alfredo according to the corresponding letter in the keyword, and recording the results in the margins of the menu. Her hand was shaking a little as the words took shape, revealing the hidden meaning.

Fettucine – Wednesday

Alfredo – Library

'The absence of the risotto reveals where he will be present. Today is Wednesday, isn't it? He'll be at the library today.'

Her heart kicked up a notch, and her stomach curled in a knot.

'Mum will be there too. She works there.'

'He's going to try to see her,' David said. She exchanged a worried glance with him, biting down on her bottom lip.

'Okay,' Dharma said, clapping his hands together. 'Let's go borrow some books I guess!'

'What about the Bloodborns?' Astari asked. 'There's still been no sign of them either.'

Rafael stepped forwards. 'Yes. Is very curious.' He shot a look at David. An understanding seemed to pass between them. She wanted to know more, but there wasn't time. She had to get to her father.

'We split up,' Rafael continued. 'I go with Dharma and the doctor to the library. You and David look for Bloodborns. Retrace our steps from last night. Maybe there is something we missed.'

David stood. 'I'll go with Essie and Dharma. Raf – you and Astari can work together, all right?'

'All right.' Astari said, giving him a slight smile. Essie

was curious about what that look meant to, but it would have to wait.

'I might be more useful hunting Bloodborns than wrangling the old man,' Dharma said, getting to his feet. David glared at him.

'Will you just do as you are told for once? Go and help Doctor Essie.'

'Fine.' He threw up his hands at Astari like a petulant teenager.

Essie folded the menu and put it back in her pocket.

'We'll meet back here, hopefully within the next hour or two.'

Dharma leaned over and picked up a small, silver blade that was lying beside his chair. She hadn't noticed it before. He tucked it down the back of his shirt. He must have been wearing a holster because it stayed in place, nestled in the small of his back. Only the barest outline, visible through the T-shirt material, hinted at its presence.

'I'm ready.' He smiled at her, and she felt warm realising that he had caught her watching him. The rest of them stood up to leave. Then David keened to one side, falling heavily. She managed to catch his arm.

'Another headache?'

He nodded, closing his eyes.

Why was it happening again? Was the other David nearby? That seemed too much of a coincidence. But what else could be causing his headaches? His skin grew pale again and his breaths were sharp and rapid. Whatever the source, he did not look to be in a fit state to go out, especially if they found the Bloodborns. She took his arm and lead him back to the settee, pushing him gently, but firmly, back down.

'I think you should stay here.'

'Yeah, you sit this one out, Sorrow,' Dharma chimed in from the back door. 'I'll take care of things.'

'I'll be fine,' he protested. But as he tried to stand again, his face folded into a mask of pain, and he slumped back, hanging his head to his knees.

'Maybe you have some kind of virus?' She placed her hand on his forehead again. 'You do feel slightly warm.'

Rafael muttered. 'It cannot be virus. Amaranthine cannot catch virus.'

She looked to Astari for confirmation. The vampire's eyes were focussed on David. She didn't seem to have heard Rafael's comment.

'Astari?' Essie prompted. 'Could it be a virus?'

Astari's gaze flicked to Essie, and she blinked a few times.

'A virus? No. Rafael is right. We are immune to all human diseases. Unless we have been reverting for some time. That is a different story.'

'Well, he's not reverting. So, what's wrong with him?' She could hear the panic rising in her voice.

Shrugging, Rafael drew the folds of his leather coat together.

'I say is not vampire thing, is time travel problem. It is to do with your science.'

Essie scowled at him, but her stomach twisted. What if Rafael was right, and it was all her fault? What if travelling to the past with her was what had made David sick? But if that were the case, why were she and Rafael perfectly fine?

Astari took up the chair beside David and patted his shoulder.

'I'm sure he will be all right again soon. I'll stay with him, Doctor Essie. You go and look for your father. You're probably the only one he will listen to.'

Essie hesitated. It was a logical offer. It made the most sense. But her feet wouldn't move. It was that feeling again. The bond between her and David. The one she couldn't understand. A feeling that was growing stronger by the day. A connection she didn't know if she could ever explain. Was this what Cecil meant about not being an island?

David leaned his head against the chair. Tiny beads of sweat glistened off his forehead. She racked her brains trying to understand what could be causing it. He waved his hand at her, his eyelids slipping closed.

'Go – I'll be fine,' he murmured.

Squashing her emotions, she nodded. Astari was right. They didn't know what condition her father would be in or how he would respond. She needed to be there when they found him.

'Okay, but we'll be back as soon as we can.'

'Let's find the old dude so we can go hunt the Bloodborns.' Dharma took out his cigarettes, a grin fixed firmly on his face as he headed for the back door again.

She adjusted her glasses. There was more she wanted to say to him. Did he feel the same way as her? Did the idea of being apart unsettle him too? She remembered again how he had held her the night before. He felt so normal. So very human. Had she imagined that something had passed between them? That he didn't want to let her go?

'I . . . David . . .' It was no use. She couldn't say it. Even if there weren't an audience. The words just wouldn't come.

'*Andiamo!*' Rafael yelled from outside.

She sighed.

'I'll take care of him,' Astari reassured her.

She nodded. That promise would have to be enough.

Chapter 12

Essie

Essie shielded her eyes with her hand as they emerged onto the main street of Mount Major, the morning sun casting a warming glow over the street and surrounds. Rafael had driven them to a nearby street where they left the car to continue on foot. She was sure the library was only a few blocks away. She set out down the footpath, the two vampires trailing her like security guards.

As she pictured a reunion with her father, her stomach twisted. The ideal scene that played out was one where she convinced him to come with her peacefully. Then they could go home and try to figure out the mess of their relationship. He had shown the lengths he would go to resurrect her mother, to rid himself of the weight of grief. But he had also seemed to have a last-minute change of heart.

In that dank church, just before he was sucked into the wormhole, he had seemed to come to his senses. The look on his face in that moment had haunted Essie. But what if arriving in the past renewed his determination to save her mother? What if he wouldn't leave with them? A shudder went down her spine, but she pressed on. He would have to come with them. She would convince him.

They passed Mount Major's only department store, and the window display caught her eye. Two mannequins stared out from behind the glass – a woman modelling a matching pink nightgown and peignoir and a man in checked pyjamas. They were enjoying a make-believe breakfast of fake coffee and plastic fruit. She stopped, her cheeks beginning to burn as another memory came crashing in on her. She had just turned thirteen. Her father led her aimlessly though the assortment of underwear and other strange lacy items, surreptitiously trying to get the attention of the female shop assistant. A well-meaning older lady, she shepherded Essie into a changing room with an armful of bras. The woman's cold fingers prodded and poked her developing chest, squishing things into place and tightening then loosening straps. Finally, the assistant declared that none of the bras were the right fit and they would start again with a different style.

It was not the last painful reminder of her mother's absence. She often suspected that adolescence would never have been smooth sailing for her, if it ever was for anyone. She was never at ease in her scarred body, always struggling in social situations. But she was sure navigating all the female firsts without anyone to guide her made it one thousand times worse. Even though her father tried, there was no one to reassure her what was normal, no one to explain how anything worked. It wasn't until much later she had to deal with any interactions with guys. The Mount Major boys had barely registered her presence, which didn't bother her at all because she was already much more interested in being in the library than going on dates. By the time she formed a tentative connection with a boy she met in first year university, she had gleaned the basic information from books. But she suspected that wasn't really the same thing as having a mother.

A voice echoed in her head.

Could it possibly make that much difference to the world if Rhonda Thornton didn't die? Will the fabric of time really fall apart because one woman lived?

She pushed the voice away. It was against the rules. Her own rules, apparently. But what if it were possible? What if she could have had her mother through all those difficult years? She shoved her hands into her pockets and her fingers closed around David's crumpled handkerchief. It was her fault he had come to the past. Her fault he was suffering now. All of it was because of her. She couldn't risk causing any more problems.

Dharma's bout of laughter broke into her thoughts, and she turned in the direction he was looking. Scanning the middle-distance, she locked eyes on a stooped man in a beige cardigan. He was standing in the middle of a large park across the road from a square, grey-brick building, bearing the sign: Mount Major Municipal Library. With the wild gesticulation of his hands, he looked to be engaged in an animated conversation, except there was no one else there. A young couple walking through the park gave him a wide berth as they lent their heads together to whisper to each other.

All her confused and angry thoughts fell away. Without consulting the vampires, she crossed the street quickly and almost broke into a run when she reached the entrance to the park. Her father did not see her coming, apparently quite lost in whatever imaginary exchange he was taking part in. She realised too late that she had no real plan about how to approach him or what she would say.

'Dad!' she cried, stopping in front of him. He stared at her for a moment, and she thought she saw a flicker of recognition pass across his face before his eyebrows drew together in a deep frown. Wrapping his arms around himself tightly, he turned his back on her.

Glancing behind, she saw that the vampires had caught up but were keeping their distance, hanging back by the park entrance. Dharma had lit up a cigarette and was leaning against the fence while Rafael stood watching her, legs planted wide, arms crossed. She took a breath and turned back to her father.

'Dad, it's me,' she said.

'You're not real,' he murmured. 'You can't be real.' He rocked himself side to side, not meeting her eyes. A pang of anxiety gripped her.

What has happened to you, Dad?

Why don't you remember me?

She had to find a way to reach him and help him overcome his confusion. Moving forwards slowly, she touched his shoulder.

'I'm real, Dad, I promise. Whatever you've been

through, I know it's a lot to handle, but I'm here and I can help you.'

He began to tremble. His hand came up to squeeze her hand.

'Is it really you, Ess?'

His face broke up and his eyes glistened. Her heart melted.

'I don't know where I am,' he said tearfully. 'I know I hurt you, somehow, but I don't . . . I can't remember what happened.'

Taking a shaking breath, she took his hand in both of hers gently.

'It's okay, Dad. I'm okay. I know it's a lot to take in, but you fell through the wormhole in the church. Do you remember that? It spat you out here in the past.'

He tilted his head uncertainly. 'But how are you here? Did it suck you in too? What happened?'

'I came here a different way.' She glanced at her wrist with the Time Weaver still securely fastened around it. There would be time to explain that later. Right now, she just had to get her father to leave the park with her quietly. She let go of his hand and held him by the shoulders, turning him to face her.

'I just remember I needed to come here. To the library.' His eyes were clouded and dark. 'I can't remember why, but it seemed so important.'

'I've come to take you home, Dad. You don't belong here. Neither of us do.'

He locked his eyes with hers and nodded briefly before his gaze drifted to the distance. She turned her head to see a woman emerging from the sliding doors of the library. Her mother. Her long dress fluttered in the breeze and her hand rested on the usual collection of wooden beads around her neck. An older lady, slightly bent at the waist, was walking beside her, and her mother laughed at something the lady said.

Her father moved out of her grasp. Heart thumping, she reached for him again, trying to clasp his elbow.

'Rhonda.' He breathed her name like a prayer, shaking Essie off and picking up his pace.

A whiff of stale cigarette hit her before she realised that Dharma and Rafael were flaking her on either side.

'No!' She extended her arms, hitting the solid wall of their respective chests. 'Just leave this to me.'

She quickly rounded in front of her father, trying to cup his face in her hands, to hold his attention.

'Dad, listen to me. You can't go over there. You can't see her.'

'But it's been so long, Ess. I just want to ... to hold her. I just want you to have her back ... I ...' He raised a shaking hand to his head, his face a mix of agitation and angst.

His desperate plea hit her like a wave crashing on a fragile shore, shaking her resolve. Then she thought of David, how unwell he was. They needed to get home. There was no other way. 'I understand. But we need to go.'

Her father's expression faltered for a moment. Then he pressed his lips together in a grim line and shook his head. 'I need to see her again.' Shoving her out of the way, he started running towards the edge of the park.

The vampires passed her, faster than she could run but still at a pace that wouldn't draw attention. Her father came to a halt outside the park entrance, right at the edge of the road. Cars whizzed in front of him.

'Please, don't hurt him,' she whispered to herself, trying to catch her breath as she ran to catch up. Her father bounced impatiently on his heels as morning traffic streamed along the road between him and her mother. There was no break in sight. Rafael reached him just as he tried to step off the curb, grabbing his cardigan and pulling him back gently. Dharma took his other arm, and they held him in place.

'Rhonda,' he yelled, trying in vain to break free of the vampires' hold.

Her mother glanced up. Everything seemed to pass in slow motion as she locked eyes with her father across the busy intersection, across the sea of time. A faint smile crossed her lips, her eyes lingering on him briefly, before she quickly turned away, giving her attention back to the old lady still beside her.

Essie caught up to the trio on the curb-side. She followed helplessly as Rafael and Dharma dragged him away from the intersection, back towards the park.

Rafael foisted him onto one of the park benches near the entrance.

'Easy!' she said, elbowing him out of the way. 'Dad, listen to me. You can't see her.' She bent to look at him, but he seemed to have gone into a trance-like state, his pupils dilated. What had happened to him? Did travelling through the wormhole affect his cognitive function? Or was he disoriented from arriving in the past unexpectedly?

She didn't have long to contemplate the questions. The atmosphere shifted, suddenly electrified with danger. The vampires both straightened, heads pivoting as their eyes scanned the park. Dharma climbed onto the bench beside her father for a better view. A second past before he lowered his gaze to Rafael and a silent communication passed between them.

'What is it?' she whispered, though she knew their alertness could only mean one thing.

'Bloodborns,' Dharma said, not turning his face to her. 'They're here.'

He jumped down from the bench and pulled her father back onto his feet.

'Time to go.' He took her father by the arm and started towards the other side of the park, where a grassed hillside led down to a narrow lane that fed a tunnel threading under the road. Essie trailed after her father, Rafael two steps behind them.

They had barely made it to the shadow of the tunnel when two figures materialised in front of them. Anna and Jono. Even though she'd seen their vampire forms before, the jolting reality of their faces still hit her hard. The bloodshot whites, the dead-eyed, black pupils, and their red lips pulled back to reveal a set of long, pointy incisors. A shudder travelled through her body. She halted, flinging out her arm to grab her father.

'I've got it!' Anna shouted, lunging at Essie's arm.

She barely dodged her grasp, stumbling backwards. A

snarl ripped through the air. Dharma rammed Anna, pinning her twisting body to the bricks. Her father was pushed sideways, landing heavily on the ground. Rafael intercepted Jono, tossing him against the underpass wall. But he rebounded, flicking a bleached dreadlock from his face and setting his sights on her.

'You!' he roared. 'Give me that!'

Essie pivoted as he launched himself at her, narrowly avoiding him as he also grabbed at her wrist. Confusion swept over her. They were after the Time Weaver.

Rafael leapt forwards again, throwing his full weight at Jono. The pair collided with a crack, spearing into the opposite wall. They fell to the ground in a tangle of limbs. Essie edged away from them. Staying low to the ground, she managed to crawl to her father's side.

Dharma jerked back, his elbow locked firmly around Anna's neck. He reached over his shoulder for the sword holstered beneath his T-shirt. She let out a low, feral sound as she clawed at the skin on his forearm, her legs kicking wildly. A glimmer of gold metal flashed in her hand. It was a slim blade, about the size of a kitchen knife.

'Get out of here!' Dharma shouted, as he tried to wrestle Anna.

A flare of adrenaline shot through Essie's system. She leapt to her feet, grabbed her father's hand, and pulled him up. He blinked rapidly, but let her lead him.

Hooking his arm over her neck, she hurried them through to the other side of the tunnel. A loud clattering echoed behind her, but she didn't dare look back as Dharma's instruction rang through her head. On the other side, there was a narrow concrete staircase that led back up to the street. Stumbling forwards one step at a time, Essie was certain that one of the Bloodborns would grab her at any moment, dragging her back down. But they made it to the curb-side, breathless and shaking.

A green sedan screeched to a halt in front of them.

'Get in,' the driver yelled through the open window. Essie pushed her glasses up her nose, trying to focus on the driver's face.

'Mum?'

Was she seeing things or was the woman behind the steering wheel really her mother? Her father let out a moan and listed heavily towards her.

'Put him in the back, Ess.' Her mother thumbed over her shoulder. Essie yanked the passenger door open and lowered her father onto the back seat, carefully folding in his legs before slamming the door and jumping into the front of the car. Her mother floored the accelerator and veered out into the traffic, narrowly missing another car.

Chapter 13

David

David took out his watch from his breast pocket and glanced at the time again. Why was it taking so long?

'Come, sit,' Astari urged him, patting the seat beside her on the settee.

He shook his head and pocketed the watch as he started pacing again.

Where are they?

It was almost midday. His resolve to remain calm was dissolving with every second that passed.

Astari tensed and David's eyes flashed towards the back door as he heard the footsteps. One familiar heartbeat was missing from the trio. Raf eased the door open, supporting the younger vampire as he limped in, swamped in Raf's leather jacket draped over his shoulders. Astari hurried to Dharma's side.

'Where's Essie?' David yelled.

'We had trouble.' Raf passed a hand through his greying curls.

'Where is she?' David repeated, hands on his hips, as he moved to block Raf's path.

'They got away. Her and her father.'

'You found him?'

'He was at library. Then Bloodborns attacked – redhead and the boy.'

'What?'

Dharma's breath was shallow and quick as Astari helped him over to the settee. Raf tossed Dharma's silver sword onto one of the chairs.

'What happened to him?' she asked. Dharma cried out, his face folding in pain as she laid his too-long body across the seat, his feet hanging off the end. Raf's jacket fell open revealing the shredded remains of Dharma's T-shirt and a jagged crimson gash. It marked his torso from his left shoulder to his right hip bone, a trail of mangled flesh. Blue bruises, like rivulets, travelled outwards from the wound.

'The redhead had a gold blade. She cut him.'

The cut looked deep, ragged at the edges. It would be fatal to a human. But Dharma was Amaranthine, and he was the younger of the pair. He was not regressing. Soon he would heal, just as David always did. Meanwhile, Essie and her father were alone, unprotected, with two Bloodborns after them.

'Where are Essie and her father now?'

Raf shrugged apologetically. 'I try to track them but their scent got lost. Then I need to move Dharma before the humans take notice. There was much blood.'

'He needs more blood. Now.' Astari's voice was choked. She leaned over Dharma, placing the back of her hand on his forehead. He moaned again, and she stroked his brow gently.

'Shhh, darling one,' she soothed him.

'Try the hospital,' David instructed. 'I'm going after Essie and her father.'

'Wait.' Raf stepped in front of him again.

'I know what you think and I know you don't approve, but so help me, Raf, if you don't get out of my way!'

Raf raised his hands in a gesture of surrender. 'I do not try stop you, *Dado*. But the Bloodborns . . . they not killing her. They want time travel watch. They know she has it.'

'What?' David recoiled. 'How could they know about the Time Weaver?'

'Someone has told them. Someone close to Essie who knows we are here.'

David caught the insinuation and shook his head. 'No. Rhonda doesn't have anything to do with this. She wouldn't betray her own daughter.'

Raf lifted his shoulders slightly. 'Why they want the watch? And why not killing her already?'

David opened his mouth to deny the assertion again, but he didn't have the time to countenance accusations of Rhonda's deception when he needed to find Essie and Gilbert. He squared his shoulders.

'I'm going to find her.' He pushed past the older vampire.

'I come with you,' Raf offered.

'No.' He threw a glance at Dharma. His body had begun

to tremble, his skin slick with sweat. 'Stay and help them. We'll meet back here before sunset.'

Raf handed him the car keys. 'Their scent finish on Victoria Road, near eastern entrance to park.'

David nodded as he donned his suit jacket.

'Be careful, *Dado*. The new Bloodborns are stronger now.'

FOLLOWING RAF'S INSTRUCTIONS, David made it to the park quickly and pulled the car to the curb. He shadowed the trail of Essie's familiar sweet clove smell, now mingled with her father's pine scent, to the eastern edge of the park. In the tunnel under the road, he caught the lingering scent of the Bloodborns – rotting flesh and decay. A pool of blood had partially soaked into the concrete. Dharma's blood. He sniffed around. The Bloodborn trail led off in the opposite direction to Essie and Gilbert. It seemed they hadn't tracked her.

Following her scent to the top of the stairs, he stopped on the side of the road where it abruptly evaporated, just as Raf had said. He paced a few metres in both directions, trying to pick up the trail again. But it was pointless. A car horn sounded behind him and his brain made the connection. Essie and Gilbert must have gotten into a car. That's why there was no further trace of them. But whose car? It could have been a taxi, he supposed.

He stood on the curb looking anxiously up and down the street for any signs of the pair. If they had gotten into a vehicle, they would be long gone. But Essie wouldn't have gone with a stranger. He turned, thinking to retrace his steps for more clues, when he ran straight into someone.

'I'm sorry,' he apologised, automatically taking a step back. An older man stood in front of him, his fair hair sprinkled with streaks of grey.

'Not to worry,' the man replied, smiling. 'My ice cream is unscathed, so that's all that matters.'

David stopped, rubbed his eyes, and blinked. The skin on his neck prickled. There was something about the man's face that was so familiar. He blinked again.

'Are you all right?' The man looked concerned, his pale brows crinkled together.

'Yes,' David stammered. 'Thanks.'

It was impossible, wasn't it? And yet . . . in his mind, he saw him again. An elderly gentleman lying in a white hospital bed, near death. Years from now and far away. Yet, as he stared into the man's eyes, all those years fell away, dissolved by the tide of time. Here he stood, alive and well.

Oh. Oh.

'Cecil!' a woman called, her voice slightly anxious. 'There you are. I thought I'd lost you.'

'Sorry, dear!' Cecil replied. 'Just ducked in to grab an ice cream while you were in the bookstore.'

The woman pursed her lips. Her hair was threaded with grey too, cut short in a stylish bob.

'Couldn't resist the Rainbow Ripple, hey?' She winked at Cecil, then turned her eyes to David.

'And who's this, then?'

'Oh – I don't actually know,' Cecil replied. 'We just ran into each other – quite literally!'

'Yes, sorry – again. I'm David.' He automatically extended his hand.

'Nice to meet you, David,' Cecil said, shaking it. 'This is my wife, Sarah.'

'Hello.' He held his smile. He knew he was staring at them for an uncomfortably long moment. But he couldn't help it. It wasn't every day he found himself in such a situation. He wished Essie were there.

Essie.

I have to find Essie.

'Look, this will sound a bit strange, but I don't suppose you saw an older man and a blonde woman come by here recently, from the park? They were probably in a hurry and . . .' his voice trailed off. What more could he say? He could hardly add that they were on the run from a pair of murderous vampires.

'I'm with the police.' He flicked his credentials in front of them briefly.

Sarah's face brightened.

'You know, I think I did. I was browsing the window display of *Canterbury's*.' She pointed in the direction of the bookstore. 'I heard a screech of tyres. When I turned around, a lady was putting the man in the backseat. Then she hopped in too.'

David nodded, his heart kicking up a beat. 'Did you happen to notice what kind of car? Was it a taxi?'

Sarah shook her head. 'It was a green sedan-type thing.'

David exhaled. The Thorntons' car. It was completely wrecked when he came upon it at the accident, but he still remembered the colour. A green sedan. Maybe Rhonda had picked them up.

'Thanks, Sarah. You've been really helpful.'

If they got into Rhonda's car, at least they were safe for now. But a vague fear played in the back of his mind at the idea of the three of them together. Rhonda had been adamant she shouldn't see Gilbert. That was one of the reasons the future Essie sent them here to get him in the first place.

'Oh good,' Sarah replied.

David nodded at the pair and took one last look, trying not to make it awkward.

'I should get going,' he said.

Cecil took a lick of his ice cream and held it aloft.

'Are you sure you don't want some ice cream? Best in town!'

Sarah punched him lightly in his rounded stomach.

'Don't encourage the young man down that path. He's still fit and healthy.'

Cecil frowned in mock hurt and licked his lips.

David pressed his palms together and angled them towards the couple.

'It was . . . lovely to meet you both.' He wanted to add that it had been quite surreal, but that wouldn't make any sense to them, so he bid them goodbye instead.

'Bye then!' Sarah chimed, waving him off.

He headed down the street, past the ice cream shop and the bookstore.

Assuming Essie and her father were in a car with Rhonda, and they were on the run from the Bloodborns, what would she do with them? Where could she hide them? They wouldn't go back to *La Fortuna*. The other Gilbert could be there. They couldn't go back to the library. How would Rhonda explain them to her colleagues? No, Essie would choose somewhere public and crowded, somewhere the Bloodborns would be reluctant to attack them.

The clang of a familiar eight-bell chime crashed into his consciousness, and he stopped to listen. Turning towards the trill, he walked a few blocks, as the midday hour rang out, until the origin of the sound came into view. The old town hall clock tower stood resplendent in its sandstone architecture. Small towns did love a nice clock tower. They always seemed to have one. In the next moment, answering bells sounded from across the city, accessing a memory pathway much older than even David himself. Church bells, calling all the faithful to mass. He chuckled lightly to himself. Could it be a sign from on high? Essie had pointed it out to them when they first arrived. Her parents were married there. The church would be busy during the mass, and it was a large building with plenty of exits. They could hide in the crowd and buy themselves some time. Plus, they had a shared history with old churches. He didn't have any better ideas, and it was as good a theory as any. He set off at a jog down the street, then threaded behind the buildings and through alleyways.

As he neared the church building, he could hear the

voices of the gathered congregation singing. Rose bushes lined the path to the entrance, abloom with pops of pink, red, and white. A few late comers straggled in the doors ahead of him, hurrying to find their seats before the service started. He straightened his tie and buttoned the top of his suit jacket as he climbed the stairs to the entrance. A tall man in a black-and-white robe handed him a printed order of service and a hymn book as he passed through the vestibule.

Inside the building, the pews were relatively well-occupied towards the front, but the numbers petered out the further back the rows went. He walked a few paces forward and slipped into a vacant spot. Depositing the order of service and hymn book onto the pew, he lifted his nose, trying to catch a familiar scent. But the song finished, and the priest instructed the congregation to take their seats. The crowd shuffled, rearranging themselves. He strained forwards, trying to recognise Essie, but many of the women's heads were covered with hats or scarves. He sat down.

Where is she? His heart ticked up a beat. Maybe his intuition had been off? Perhaps they hadn't come to the church. Rhonda could have dropped them somewhere else. He wished desperately that they had mobile phones. He inhaled once more and finally caught it. Faint but detectable. Sweet cloves. He scanned the pews in front of him again, finally spotting a twist of blonde hair. As if sensing his gaze, Essie turned her head towards him. He caught her eyes and a flicker of understanding passed between them. Her shoulders relaxed, and she leaned in, whispering to the woman beside her. It was Rhonda, her dark hair partially covered in a brightly coloured scarf. David made out her father sitting on Essie's other side.

The priest murmured a few words of welcome, then a prayer. When the organ started up for the next song and the congregation rose, David made his way down the aisle and edged into Essie's row. Rhonda let him slide past her. Essie reached for his hand, interlacing her fingers with his. A warm feeling spread up his arm and to his chest.

'You found me.'

'Always,' he replied without even thinking. He braced himself as she stared up at him for a long moment, her eyes a deep blue behind her perennially smudged glasses, and her expression hard to decipher. Gilbert cleared his throat, breaking the spell.

'Why are we at mass, Ess? We don't believe any of this rubbish!'

Essie shushed him with her finger over her lips.

'I told you, Dad. We were waiting for David.'

'I want to go home.'

Essie turned back to David, her face tense. 'He's confused. He doesn't seem to understand what's happened. I don't know what's wrong with him.'

'He's been through a lot. Let's get out of this church and go somewhere quiet.'

'Where though? Mum's meant to be at the restaurant already. Anna and Jono attacked us in the park. Dharma and Rafael fought them. We only just escaped.'

A vision of Dharma's mangled torso formed in his mind.

'Dharma was hurt. Rafael and Astari are looking after him.'

'What?' She responded a little too loudly, drawing a dark look from a woman in the row in front of them.

'Let's get out of here,' he said again, reaching around Essie to take Gilbert by the elbow. Essie ushered her mother out into the aisle as he manoeuvred Gilbert behind them.

The robed man at the door gave them a disapproving look as they shuffled past him and out into the carpark.

'Thank you for rescuing us, Mum. I'll figure things out with Dad, I promise.' She put an arm around her father's shoulder.

Rhonda pulled the scarf from her head, looking at Gilbert with a sad, longing glance. 'I know I wasn't meant to see him, but I thought you might need help when I saw him at the park.'

She dug around in her large canvas handbag and retrieved a set of keys, keeping her gaze down as she fiddled with her wedding ring.

'I don't know how to say goodbye to you for a second time, Ess,' she said, pressing her lips together. 'It was hard enough before in the motel.' Her eyes filled with tears as she gently caressed her daughter's face and then leaned forwards, embracing her tightly. 'Whatever else happens,' she whispered. 'I am so glad I got to see you.'

Essie's eyes glistened.

'I . . . I'll love you forever, Mum.'

When at last they separated, Essie stood watching as Rhonda rushed away to her car without looking back.

Pushing her glasses onto the top of her head, she wiped at the silent tears that had fallen onto her cheeks. David clenched his hand at his thigh, his breath catching.

'Are you . . . are you all right?' he asked.

Gilbert tapped her on the shoulder. 'I want to go home.'

She sighed and replaced her glasses. 'I'm fine.' She took her father firmly by the elbow. 'Let's get back to the others.'

Chapter 14

Essie

David flashed his police credentials at the bus driver while she stood behind her father, gripping his arm. The driver motioned them on free of charge, and they rode the few stops back to the library where he had left the car. It seemed like it was early afternoon, judging by the sun overheard. Pale clouds gathered on the horizon and the air felt humid. Her father kept asking where they were going. His breaths were laboured and erratic and he complained of having a headache. Was he experiencing the same symptoms as David? Why was it affecting the two of them and not her or Rafael? Her father still seemed confused. He knew who she and her mother were, but he didn't seem to know much else. What could be wrong? She tried to keep her worry at bay as she found a seat and steered him into it. He sat down, his eyes fixed out the window as the bus whirred off.

'They were going to get blood for Dharma, for his injury, but they should be back by now,' David explained quietly, standing in the aisle beside her. She wrinkled her nose at him. The thought of Dharma's injuries made her queasy and brought another pang of guilt to her chest. He had been injured protecting her and her father.

'Was he badly hurt?'

'He'll be fine,' David assured her.

She took in his familiar face. He still looked weary. There was tension evident around the set of his jaw, his eyes slightly cloudy. But for reasons having nothing to do with any logical thought process, being with him made her feel like she could breathe again. Her shoulders dropped and the knot of anxiety in her stomach started to ease.

The bus stopped outside the library and they walked the short distance back to the car. Her father jabbered away the whole drive back to the house, but it was only fragments of sentences and nothing discernible. She exchanged a concerned look with David. What if her father's behaviour wasn't just shock? What if going through the wormhole had done irreparable damage to his brain?

The thought returned to her again.

This is all my fault.

Leaving her mother at the church was like ripping her heart in two again. She knew what she had to do, that it was the right thing to do, but it was getting harder to tell herself that as more and more things seemed to go wrong. Dharma hurt, her father troubled, the Bloodborns still on the loose.

She had to stay focussed. At least they had found her father. And David's headache had gone. Dharma would have blood and heal, then they could deal with the Bloodborns and get home. Maybe once her father was back in the right time, he'd snap out of it.

When they arrived at the house, David slid the door open, and she led her father inside. It was dark and quiet. The air around her swirled and Rafael appeared. She jumped before rounding on him in anger.

'Rafael, I swear to God, if you do that again, I won't be responsible for my actions! I am not in the mood for your tricks!'

He flicked on a light. His mouth curved down solemnly, and his eyes were almost panicked. She had never seen him look like that before.

'Raf, what's wrong?' David slid the back door closed behind them.

Rafael hesitated as he pushed a grey curl from his forehead.

'It is Dharma. *Il suo sangue maledetto.* How you name it in English?' His words had left him again. She had no idea what he was saying, but whatever it was, it didn't seem like good news. David's expression confirmed her fears.

'Cursed blood, or rotted blood,' he said slowly. 'In English, you would perhaps call it bloodrot.'

That definitely did not sound good.

'What is bloodrot?' she asked, her eyes wide. David cupped his chin, rubbing the five o'clock shadow that had emerged.

A terrifying wail rang out from one of the rooms down the hall. David flinched. She shuddered, turning her head towards the sound.

'But how, Raf? You said here hasn't been bloodrot for...'

'Centuries,' Rafael finished. 'I have not seen for centuries. But the chest wound . . . the Bloodborns have infected him somehow.' He dropped his gaze, his grey brow furrowing.

Her father started rambling again, his words confused and scattered.

'Shh, Dad,' she said, helping him over to the settee and settling him comfortably against the floral pillows. She turned back to them.

'Okay, so how do we help Dharma? What should we do?'

The two vampires would not meet her eyes. David shifted his weight onto his heels and slipped his hands into his pockets. She looked from him to Rafael and back again.

'Nothing,' Rafael said at last.

'But we must be able to do something,' she sighed. 'Does he need more blood? I could give him blood if it would help?' She shrugged off her jacket and began rolling up her sleeve.

'No!' they snapped in unison. She froze. David's face softened a little as he moved towards her. Placing his hand gently on her elbow, he smiled tightly.

'You must stay away from Dharma. If you are near him, if any human gets near him in the first stages, he won't be able to stop himself from feeding. But no amount of blood can heal him. Bloodrot makes Amaranthine like rabid dogs. Erratic, aggressive.'

She swallowed hard and glanced back at her father. He

was sitting with his legs pulled up tightly, fidgeting with the buttons on the front of his cardigan and muttering something to himself.

'You've seen this before?' she asked, turning back to David.

He shook his head.

'I have,' Rafael murmured. 'But not for long time.'

Essie pressed her lips together, fighting back the tears stinging her eyes. How could this have happened?

'There must be something you can do.'

Rafael scratched his head.

'Nika mentioned something about a cure . . . long ago. But it was story. No proof.'

'How long does he have?'

Rafael shrugged. 'Difficult to say. Hours. Perhaps longer. Astari is with him.'

A chill came over Essie, permeating her muscles and bones. She hugged herself, running her hands up and down her arms.

This is not right. Dharma was trying to help.

Another cry resonated from the hallway, a strangled, choking noise. She squeezed her lids closed against the awful sound. It died abruptly. When she opened her eyes, Dharma's face was inches from hers, his mouth stretched wide, a slash of red. The handsome, carefree young man she had met the day before was gone. In his place was a snarling, savage monster baring down on her. His white fangs glistened, his eyes were dead and unseeing. Rafael and David's vice-like hold on both of his arms was the only thing preventing him from advancing on her. She stumbled backwards, shaking.

'Dharma.'

Astari materialised in the space between her and the vampire, begging for his attention, whispering words of comfort. Essie couldn't see her face, but she could hear the emotion in her voice. Dharma's expression relaxed, and he sagged back, deflating.

'I'm sorry,' he sobbed. 'So sorry.'

Astari stroked the sweat-slick hair away from his face.

'Stay here,' David ordered as the three of them dragged his limp body away.

Lights danced in front of her eyes. She clutched at her chest and tried to steady herself, the world beginning to spin. Outside, the sky darkened as the clouds cast long shadows across the porch. A clap of thunder broke overhead, and rain drops hit the tin roof with a gentle patter. She staggered to the settee numbly, sinking down beside her father. One thought kept coming back to her, over and over again.

This is not right.

Nothing about this is right.

She rocked herself slowly. The skin on her scarred hand tingled, and she scratched at it absently, not noticing it become a series of red, angry welts. Her mother's face floated in her mind's eye, beautiful and vibrant and alive. The emotions that she had been tenuously holding in check beat against the cage of her ribs as she fought to suppress the heavy ache in her heart. The ache that had been there since she first saw her mother on her doorstep.

The ache that was solidifying by the minute, hardening into something else.

In her mind, memories played like movies. Her mother smiling. Her mother reading to her. Dancing in the kitchen together at *La Fortuna*, her father with his spaghetti moustache. A collage of their life together. Of the life that was lost. Of all that should have been.

She wasn't sure how long she sat rocking – minutes, hours. Time wasn't measurable. It sped up and slowed down inside the echoes of Dharma's spasmodic cries, echoing through the house. The vampires tended to him and she could tell his condition was getting worse. David came out once or twice, trying to get her to eat something. But the thought of food made her nauseous. Her father kept muttering as he held his head in his hands, indiscernible utterances and sounds.

Daylight faded into the blanket of night and the rain picked up in intensity. A gutter above the back door, unprepared for the downpour, overflowed, water cascading over the patio in an unrelenting stream. The rain storm that had come through the night of the car accident, so long ago, was now just a few hours away. Every time the thunder clapped, her father cringed. She took his hand in hers, held it in her lap. She'd never noticed it before, but the shape of his fingers and the curve of his nails were exactly like hers. She thought about how she'd judged him for his weakness. Unable to understand the way he allowed his emotions to rule him, the things that love had driven him to do. But now the truth crystallised in her mind with a gut-wrenching clarity. They weren't so very different.

She leaned towards him. 'It will be all right, Dad.'

Yanking back her shirt sleeve, she stared down at the Time Weaver. The tiny blue lights winked at her, cycling on and off. It was a singular technology biologically mapped to her alone. It gave the power to her and her alone. That had to mean something. And the question that had bothered her from the beginning hung suspended in her mind now, as harsh as a naked lightbulb.

Why would I do this to myself?

Why give me this chance, if not to change everything?

I can change everything.

When she stood up, the ache that had threatened to strangle her heart moments before was gone. It had been replaced by something else more durable, unbreakable. Grasping her father by his elbow, she pulled him to his feet and straightened his cardigan. Dharma's feral cry rang out again, but she turned away from it.

'Come on,' she whispered. She led him quietly out the back door and into the drizzly darkness.

Chapter 15

David

David and Rafael held Dharma on either side while he thrashed about. He wasn't sure how long they had been restraining him. He had been concentrating his full strength on keeping the younger vampire pinned to the ground as his limbs contorted and flailed.

Raf had once told him a story about bloodrot. He had followed the trail of some Bloodborns to a village in rural France. The Bloodborns were already dead when he arrived, killed by another Amaranthine. But they had infected her with contaminated blood in the scuffle. He found her holed up in a barn, surrounded by exsanguinated corpses. The humans she had vowed to protect were now casualties, her promise obliterated by the red mist. She lay in the hay, gnashing her teeth, foam around her mouth. In the end, she had begged for death.

David shuddered as he thought about how narrowly he had stopped Dharma when he lunged at Essie. If he had succeeded, she would have been torn apart before she even knew what was happening. The thought pierced him, twisting like a knife.

Astari knelt behind Dharma, cradling his head. Her dark hair fell heavily over her shoulders as she leaned down to him, humming soft words into his ear. His face glistened with sweat and his distended fangs were glaringly white against the caramel of his skin. After a few moments, he stilled. His body sagged and his eyelids slid closed.

'You can let go,' Astari said, her voice barely above a whisper. 'I think this is the paralytic stage. He shouldn't be any threat to the humans now.' Astari had also seen bloodrot before, but like Raf, not for at least a hundred years. They were both at a loss as to how he was infected.

Gingerly releasing Dharma's arm, he edged back slightly. Raf followed suit, staying close. Dharma twitched and shuddered, but his head fell limply to the side as a trickle of drool escaped his lips. Astari wiped at it with the hem of her shirt.

Silence descended on the room, and David sat back on his knees, wiping the back of his hand across his brow. Astari cocked her head towards the kitchen and frowned.

'It is too quiet,' she said softly.

He attuned his ears. There was no sound in the other room. Only the absence of the two beating hearts. Raf registered it at the same moment and nodded. When he raced into the lounge room, it was empty. Outside, the sky was dark, rain pelting down.

'They're gone,' he said, returning to the bedroom.

'Go. I'll stay here.'

He took in Astari's face. Stoically dry-eyed until now, she was crying freely, the tears streaming down her cheeks.

'I'm so sorry, Astari. If I'd known . . .'

She shook her head. Taking up both of Dharma's hands, she folded them gently across his bare chest and stroked his sweaty forehead.

'There's nothing we can do now except be with him to the end. You must find the doctor and her father and bring them back. We were all drawn here for a reason. My heart tells me there is more yet to come.'

He nodded. 'I'll be back.'

Dharma's features were relaxed now, almost as if he were sleeping. Glancing at Raf once more, he left.

There was no Bloodborn scent in the house. They would have sensed them if they had been there. Essie and Gilbert had left of their own accord. But why? And why wouldn't she tell him? Didn't she trust him? Dharma's condition had upset her. He had seen it in her wary eyes as she sat on the couch, pale and silent. But she had to know he would never let anything happen to her. Grabbing his jacket, he ran out the back door. Rain sluiced across his face. He looked up and down the street, but there was no sign of her or Gilbert. He lifted his nose to catch their scent, but the deluge had washed everything away. The car was still parked against the curb. Essie didn't drive. So they couldn't have gotten too far yet. Where were they going?

He turned the question over in his mind as he fished the keys from his pocket and slid behind the wheel of the car. He felt for his watch and checked the time. Close to 9:00 p.m. The truth settled over him with certainty, a stone mass settling in his stomach. There was only one obvious answer. She had been fighting it since they arrived. Forcing her rationality to prevail. Tamping down her emotions, refusing to discuss it. She was desperate to stick to the rules, desperate not to succumb to the feelings that had driven her father to betray her. She had struggled to overcome the fear at war with her faith in herself. Now, it seemed, that fear had won out.

He turned over the engine and steered the car out to the main street of Mount Major, turning back towards the highway. Pressing the accelerator down firmly, he prayed he'd be able to find the turn-off to Ridgeway Lane in the stormy darkness, and that he'd be fast enough to beat Essie and Gilbert to the scene.

Chapter 16

Essie

Essie couldn't remember exactly what time they had left the restaurant the night of the accident. She was only eight years old. She didn't pay attention to things like that. But it was nine forty-five now. Hopefully, *La Fortuna*'s dinner service wouldn't be over yet. Hopefully, she could still find her parents there. Warn them somehow. Change everything.

But they had to walk and progress was slow with her father by her side. He kept stopping every few feet, still muttering away under his breath, occasionally holding his head as if in pain. She glanced behind them, expecting David to catch up at any moment. Once he realised they were gone, he would come after them. She was sure of it. Her heart hurt at the thought, at how worried he would be. She pushed the feeling away as the rain picked up. The damp was soaking through her jacket and the temperature kept falling. She shivered against the cold. They finally rounded the corner to the shopping centre. Most of the shops were closed except for the supermarket.

Letting go of her father's hand, she ran to the window of *La Fortuna*. She peered through the glass, but it was dark inside. There was no movement. She banged her fist on the door and shouted. No response.

Damn it. Where are they?

Her father caught up, stood next to her.

'Why are we here, Ess? At the restaurant?' His face was lined with confusion. At least he recognised the restaurant. But how much did he understand about what was happening?

'We have to hurry. They've left already. But we can catch up, warn them somehow.'

There was a taxi rank near the front of the supermarket. She ushered her father towards it. An elderly woman was exiting the only car in the rank. Essie tapped on the driver's side window, and he rolled it down.

'We need to go to the Ridgeway Lane turn-off. Can you take us?'

He scratched his head. 'Ridgeway Lane? Where's that?'

'It's on the highway, back towards Feldham.'

'Hang on, love.' He punched a few buttons on a keyboard mounted to the dashboard and turned back. 'Okay, I've got time before my next job.'

She opened the rear door and pushed her father into the back seat. Climbing in behind him, she clicked both of their seatbelts in place. As the driver moved off, she glanced at his clock radio. Almost 10:00 p.m.

She silently willed the driver to go faster, searching for her parents' sedan on the road ahead. It was difficult in the dark. Rain obscured the windscreen. The restaurant closed at 9:00 p.m., but it took a little while to pack up. If they had just left the restaurant, the car should be on the highway, a few minutes ahead of them. They came up on another vehicle and her heart leapt. But it was a white hatchback. The taxi driver overtook it, pressing on into the darkness.

Where are they?

The driver pointed at a road sign. 'This it, love?' He slowed and put on his indicator.

She peered out the window, just able to make out the reflective words on the sign. Ridgeway Lane.

'Yes, that's it!' Eucalyptus trees swayed on either side of the road, their leaves shimmering with rain drops.

'Stop here.' She glanced out the back window of the taxi. There was still no sign of her parents' car, but at least they were in the right spot. They could wait on the side of the road and flag them down.

'Are you sure this is it, love? There's nothing here. It's pretty wet outside.' The driver looked at her over his shoulder, his face concerned.

'It's fine,' she said, pushing open the back door and grabbing her father's hand. He shuffled across the seat and followed her out.

The front passenger window rolled down and the driver leaned across the car.

'Okay, that'll be $13.35.'

Argh!

She still didn't have any money. Her father tugged her sleeve. She turned to him, impatient. 'What, Dad?'

He held out a twenty-dollar note. She took it gratefully and passed it to the driver. He handed her some change before giving her a puzzled look then turning in a circle and driving off back into the darkness.

She glanced around, trying to orient herself while rain slashed at her face, fogging up her glasses. The police had never been able to work out for sure what caused their car to run off the road near Ridgeway Lane. But it was likely a wild animal. Kangaroos and wombats caused accidents all the time, especially on wet country roads. Her father had braked before he swerved. She had heard the wheels screeching on the road. She would wait for the car to round the bend and stop them. They couldn't run off the road if the car was stopped.

Rain kept coming down. Her clothes were saturated now, and she struggled to stop her teeth from chattering together. Her father was drenched through as well. She searched around for some shelter.

'Come over here. We'll wait under this tree until we see the car.'

Shivering, they huddled against the tree trunk. The time travel rules ran through her mind.

Don't travel to the same place twice.

Don't meet past versions of yourself.

Don't change past events.

She was possibly breaking all three at once just by being there. But this was her only chance. She had to take it. She crouched low, pulling her father down next to her.

A noise came from behind them. The cracking of a stick under foot, followed by a low growl. Her head swivelled towards the sound, but she couldn't make out anything in the darkness. Her father began to mutter again, and she clamped her hand over his mouth to muzzle the sound. She held her breath, but it was now completely silent now, except for the beating rain.

The whir of a car engine drew her attention back to the road. In the darkness, she could only make out the headlights. But it had to be her parents' car. They had to have been only minutes behind the taxi. The atmosphere rippled around her, humming, reverberating. Her father crouched down, folding his arms over his head.

'Make it stop, make it stop,' he cried. She squatted beside him, her hand on his back.

'Make what stop? What's wrong?' She stroked his shoulder, his cardigan now saturated.

'Found you again.' The voice in the darkness was familiar, angry. 'Do you think it was wise to come out here unprotected?'

She tried to stand but stumbled and staggered forwards. Gravel bit into her hands and knees.

What was *she* doing here? How did she even know this place? Had she been following them?

'Anna, listen,' she said shakily. But as quickly as the words left her mouth, Anna's arm circled her throat. She choked, the air coming in gasps.

Anna ran a hand over her head, stroking her hair.

'No, thanks. I've listened to your whining voice enough to last a lifetime.'

In the distance, headlights bore down on them, edging closer and closer. Her father clung to her leg, moaning garbled words.

'I didn't think I could ever hate you more than I already did, but then you sent me back here, back to this hellish past, with *him*.'

Essie struggled against Anna's grip, but her arm was like stone and she was in a chokehold. Anna's clothes smelled of blood, metallic and musty.

'Then she found us, and everything became clear again.'

Anna spun Essie around, her hands planted firmly on her shoulders. She made a soft sucking sound as she licked her lips.

'I'm not allowed to kill you. It's too soon. But I can drink you. Just a little taste. I'm desperate for something fresh.'

Essie struggled to think clearly, adrenaline spiking through her veins. Anna pushed her head to the side, then struck quickly, like a coiled snake. There was a sharp sting, followed by the pressure of Anna's mouth. Warm, sticky liquid trickled down her neck.

From the corner of her eye, she could see the car. It was nearly on them. Whether in response to Anna biting her or something else, her father roused and stood up. He shuffled in a circle, his hands over his ears, his eyes unfocussed.

'My head. My head hurts,' he cried, backing away.

Essie strained against Anna's hold, reaching for him. A few more steps and he would be on the road. But her head was swimming, her vision blurry. She managed to brush his sleeve with her fingertips before he slipped out of her reach.

He stumbled backwards onto the road. The car drove towards him. She held her breath, bracing for the impact, expecting the moment the hood would strike his body. Brakes squealed on the wet bitumen, the smell of burning rubber permeated the air. But between one blink and the next, her father vanished from the road. There was a sickening, cracking noise and Anna went limp, collapsing at Essie's feet. Strong arms closed around her, and her legs trembled. She leaned into the familiar, solid weight of David's chest as he pulled her away from the road. In the distance, tail-lights blurred in the rain as the car swerved wildly. It jerked suddenly to the right, tumbled over on its roof once, then again, before colliding with a tree trunk and coming to a sudden halt.

Chapter 17

David

David pressed his folded handkerchief firmly onto Essie's bloodied neck.

'Hold that there.'

Running his hands over her, he quickly checked for any other signs of injury or broken bones. He sighed. She was unharmed, apart from the neck wound.

The Thorntons' car rested against the solid trunk of a eucalypt on the other side of the road, a few hundred metres down from them. Smoke streamed from the damaged hood and a shiny liquid spewed out from underneath. That was what had caused the fire. Leaking fuel. He remembered the report from the accident investigators. A spark had caught from the overhead power lines on the spilled petrol.

'Mum, Dad,' Essie screamed, trying to free herself of his grip. He held fast to her.

'You can't, Essie. We have to go. I'll be here soon – the

other me. And you and Gilbert also cannot meet your past selves. Remember the rules your mother told us.'

'No,' she cried. 'We can't leave them. We can save them.'

Her face contorted with pain. He had to get her out of there. All his preternatural instincts were telling him they had to run.

Gilbert stood in the middle of the road, oblivious to the downpour around him. The car had swerved to avoid him. He had been the reason for the accident. He dragged Essie across the road and grabbed Gilbert with his free hand. She kicked against him as he bundled them both into the back of the car and shut the door. He was in the driver's seat less than a second later, slamming the locks down, preventing her escape. He started the engine and turned the car back towards Mount Major. As they drove away, he heard it again, the sound he had tried to block from his memory for the better part of twenty-five years. A little girl, crying in the darkness. Eight-year-old Essie trapped in the back of the Thorntons' wrecked car.

'Please,' she begged from the backseat. 'Please. You have to save her. Please!'

Gilbert beat the side of his head with a closed fist.

'Make it stop, make it stop!'

It took every part of his resolve to keep his eyes on the road, his hands white knuckling the steering wheel. Eventually, Essie quietened down. When he glanced in the rearview mirror, she was huddled in the corner of the car, her knees drawn up to her chest.

He wanted to say he was sorry. There were so many things he wanted to say. But he knew none of it would make her feel better.

'Keep the pressure on your neck.'

Gilbert curled forwards, his head in his hands. Did he understand what had just happened? David wasn't sure he understood himself. Anna was at the scene of the accident. He had incapacitated her by snapping her neck. She wouldn't be down long, but he couldn't dispose of her permanently without a blade. So many questions raced through his mind. How had Anna found Essie and her father? It was a remote, dark country road. How would she have even known to look there? And where was Jono? Raf's words came back to him. Someone else was helping the Bloodborns. They had to be. Someone who knew about the past, and perhaps the future as well.

They drove the rest of the way back to the house in silence, save for Essie's occasional sniffs. He parked and went around to open her door. When he reached for her, she allowed herself to be drawn out of the car.

Raf stood at the back door. David listened for a moment. There were only two heartbeats inside the house. Only two vampires. He met Raf's eyes and his heart sank as he saw the confirmation in them. Dharma was gone. He led Essie and Gilbert inside and settled them on the settee. Both their clothes were still soaked. He turned on the wall-mounted heater and draped a blanket over them.

Raf was waiting on the porch. He stepped outside and slid the door closed behind him.

'Where they go?'

'She went after her mother, trying to stop the accident. But it didn't work. Her father wandered onto the road, and the car veered to miss him. The accident happened anyway.'

Raf frowned. 'So, the old man caused accident first time, or now the past has changed?'

He shrugged.

'I don't know how it works, Raf. Either way, she's just lost her mother again. And her father is . . .'

Gilbert had leaned his head against the back of the couch, his eyes closed, his hands resting loosely in his lap. At least he seemed a little calmer now.

'How is Astari?'

Raf's shoulders rose and fell.

'Not good. But she has survived loss before. She survive this.'

'This is different, though, Raf. Dharma was her pair.'

'I know.'

He did know. He had lost his pair. The person he had been with for decades, centuries. How did one survive that kind of grief? Raf had never gotten over Nika's loss. He had just learnt to live with it, somehow.

'There is blood in fridge. Leftover from hospital supplies.'

'Thanks. How are you?'

Raf rocked his hand back and forth.

'I was good when we fought Bloodborns in park. I take some refreshment.'

David nodded. *The Bloodborns.*

'Raf, Anna was there on the side of the road. She

attacked Essie. Bit her neck. Some blood loss, but she'll be all right. The other one, Jono, wasn't with her. I snapped Anna's neck, but without a blade ...'

Raf cupped his hand under his chin thoughtfully.

'I'm beginning to agree with your theory. Someone is helping them.'

'*Un maestro,*' Raf murmured.

A puppet master.

The question was, who? Raf already said he suspected Rhonda, but David just couldn't see it. What reason could she have had to betray her daughter? And now she was dead, wasn't she, killed in the accident they had just witnessed? Her father could still be working with the Bloodborns, but he seemed too disoriented to be of any use. Unless it was all an act. The hooded figure in his dreams burst into his mind. Both he and Astari had had similar dreams of that person. Could the ancient creator of the Bloodborns still be on the loose, as Astari feared? Was it him lurking behind the scenes, calling all the plays?

But before they could find out, there were more immediate concerns.

'We should leave here. The Bloodborns must have been tracking us. They probably know about this place.'

Raf lifted his chin in unspoken agreement.

'We will need to dispose of Dharma's body first.'

'Astari prepare him now. She bathe him.'

He attuned his ears and the gentle hum of Astari's voice came to him, accompanied by the sound of running water. It was ghostly, eerie. His eyes went to Essie. She was shivering, her bloodstained and wet clothes clinging to her. He stepped back inside.

'Essie, let's get you both changed out of those wet things before you catch a chill. I don't want you to get sick.'

Essie focussed her gaze on him, her eyes bloodshot but steadfast. Something about her gaze unsettled him.

'I don't care what you want.'

Chapter 18

Essie

David fixed his iridescent eyes on her. She could have lost herself in those eyes, in the paradox of his existence – young and old at the same time, strong but safe. A part of her longed to be lost. But another part, a damaged, broken part, was wailing inside, still refusing to give in.

This is all my fault.

She was the reason they had been on the road tonight. The reason Anna was in the past and had tracked them there. The reason her father had stumbled into the path of the car. The reason her mother had died. Everything was clear now. It had all begun with her.

'Essie, after Raf and I find Anna and Jono, we can go home. That was our mission here. The mission your mother gave us.'

She reached for Cecil's tiny bicycle charm inside her shirt and clasped it in her fist.

I don't want to be an island, Cecil.

But it's too hard.

It hurts too much.

The charm was cold in the palm of her hand. She let it go, then peeled her wet cuff away from her wrist. The Time Weaver lit up.

'I know what my mum said, but she's wrong.'

Her voice sounded hollow and far away to her, as if it belonged to someone else. She stood up and backed herself away from David, into the corner of the room.

'Essie.'

The way he said her name carried an edge of warning.

'What are you doing?'

She turned from him, hunching over the Time Weaver.

'My mum isn't...'

The words broke off, her throat suddenly closing.

Mum isn't anything anymore.

The living, breathing woman she had met for the first time only two days ago was dead, again. Her sparkling eyes were shut forever. She was now lying lifeless, on the side of the road, near Ridgeway Lane. And the car would have caught fire and seared the skin off her own eight-year-old body, trapped in the back seat. And she'd have to live through the nightmare of it all over. Growing up without her. Stumbling through adolescence on her own. It happened twenty-five years ago, but it was also happening today, kilometres away. How was she supposed to wrap her brain around that? The past and present all happening at once. And how was she supposed to walk away? She squared her shoulders, trying to hold her body rigid and stop the trembling as it spread through her bones.

'Mum didn't understand the first thing about quantum mechanics.'

'But you do. And sometime in the future, you make even greater strides in the technology and invent the Time Weaver. And that future you gave your mother specific instructions about time travel. Your rules were very clear.'

His face was expectant, hopeful.

The rules.

Tangible. Objective. Logical. Logic is the foundation of all scientific reasoning.

I am a scientist.

I am logical.

Rafael stepped towards her. She flinched. David stretched out his arm, cautioning the older vampire to keep back.

I want to be logical.

The pain inside her chest beat against the cage of her ribs, robbing all her other senses of the ability to function.

But logic is what got you here in the first place.

Your insatiable longing for scientific knowledge.

You had to solve Zion's Loop.

You couldn't let it be.

She dragged in a ragged breath and tensed her muscles against the force of her regret as it threatened to burst her open.

'But my mother's dead. I just watched her die. Again. And my father . . .'

She glanced at him, staring straight ahead, his eyes unseeing.

'His brain is fried – probably because he fell through a wormhole. The one I created.'

David raised his hands in a gesture of surrender. But she was not in a mood to take prisoners. The river of anguish coursing through her swept up her grief and guilt and threatened to break its banks.

'And now I know that all of it is *my* fault. Everything that's happened is because of *me*. Since the very beginning. I caused the car accident by coming back here. And everything else flowed from there. My work on Zion, my father's disappearance, Sabine – even Anna – if only I had been kinder to her. Maybe . . . maybe. I had so many chances to change things. And now Dharma . . .'

Oh, Dharma.

His beautiful, boyish face, completely transfigured by bloodrot. He got infected protecting her and her father. And now he was dead too.

'We don't know that us being here is the reason your mother died, Essie. You once told me that time is complicated. There is still so much we don't understand.'

His smile was gentle, reassuring. But she hated it when he used her words against her, her own logic. Especially when he could never fathom what it meant. He might be over a hundred years old, but he didn't understand the physics. And he didn't understand the pain. The terrible pain of guilt that ached through every bone and muscle and had engulfed her brain like a vicious black fog. No one understood that.

'I know what I've done.'

'No, Essie. You are not responsible for all of this.'

151

'The Bloodborns wouldn't have even been interested in me if it weren't for my work on Zion's Loop. Isn't that right, Rafael?'

The taciturn vampire angled his chin up, his sharp eyes never leaving hers.

'See,' she laughed but it was a crude, dead sound. 'He has nothing to say. Because he knows I'm right.'

'Raf . . .'

Rafael made a rumbling sound as he folded his arms over his chest.

'*Dado* is right. We go back home,' he said at last. 'This time travel is not natural.'

He was right about that. It wasn't natural. It was a huge mistake. But at least it was one she could try to fix. She held the Time Weaver closer to her face so she could focus on the tiny numbers.

'I am going back. But not home.'

'Essie . . .' The warning again. But she didn't care. She was past that.

'If Mum was able to bring us twenty-five years into the past, I can go back two hours. Two hours is nothing. But it's everything. With two hours, I can start again. We all can.'

David raised his eyebrows at her as understanding dawned on him. But when it came down to it, would he try to stop her? Could he?

'This isn't the way,' he pleaded. 'We've already broken the first rule. We should never have been at the crash site tonight. Remember the second rule: you cannot revisit the same place twice. We have no idea what will happen if you do. Please, listen to me.'

She manipulated the settings on the bracelet, spinning the dial to wind back the minutes and hours. Time evaporated under her fingertips. She locked in the date and time and synced it.

'Essie!'

She closed her ears. She didn't want to hear his calm advice. She didn't want to hear that it was wrong. The beating inside her ribcage intensified, pummelling her with pent-up anguish that set every nerve ending ablaze.

Please make the pain stop.

Please let me be able to breathe again.

'Please, Essie.'

She felt her mother's arms around her, remembering how she had squeezed her so tightly. Her voice, her laugh. The glint in her dark eyes.

The powerful tide of grief washed over her, and her body convulsed under its weight. A brand-new wound opened over the old one, tearing up the toughened scars of the last twenty-five years. The long curse of time's shadow darkened her mind, crushing her, and she struggled to draw enough oxygen with every breath.

'I can fix this.'

David was suddenly in front of her, his hands anchored on her arms.

'You're lying to yourself, Essie. You know this isn't right.'

She trembled with a forced laugh and pushed his hands away.

'That's rich, coming from you! You lie all the time. Your whole life is a lie. You live amongst us, but you're nothing like us. You don't know what it's like. You've existed for so long that you've forgotten what it is to be human and vulnerable and scared.'

He shook his head, his eyes wide.

'I assure you, that is not the case. I still feel all the human emotions. I sometimes wish I didn't. This life would be so much easier. But I do feel – joy, loss, happiness, and sorrow. All of it.'

He hesitated, frowning at her.

'And right now, I feel afraid. Not because you might tear a hole in the fabric of reality. But because I am afraid to lose you. I don't want to lose you. I can't.'

His eyes bored into her. Cerulean blue. She blinked. The meaning of his words took hold of her. A tiny hole pierced through her agony, a pinprick of light in the darkness of the hurt inside her.

I am afraid to lose you.

He was afraid? Because of her?

Then he moved. She had no time to react. He knocked her off kilter as he whooshed away from her. She overbalanced, stumbling back against the wall. By the time she righted herself, he was standing next to Rafael, holding the Time Weaver. He slipped it into his jacket, out of sight.

She stared down into her empty hand and slid slowly down the wall, folding inwards as her arms wrapped tightly around herself. Sobs racked her body. She gripped her arms tighter, trying to hold herself together, to stop the pain from tearing her apart. One heartbeat passed, then

David's arms were around her too. He drew her gently against his chest. Air came into her lungs at last, and when she exhaled, she let out a low rasping cry. It was messy and ugly and awful. It was everything she always wanted to keep hidden inside herself, everything no one else should see. The pain surged through her, but he didn't let go. His touch was tender but steadfast. He kept holding onto her, all the disparate parts of her, drawing them back together. She relaxed into his embrace and closed her eyes. She was safe.

Chapter 19

David

David couldn't remember the last time he'd held someone the way he was holding Essie now. The slight weight of her in his arms, her scent. Something inside him shifted and curled, bowing with her as she sobbed. She shook with a ferocity that made her teeth chatter. She was icy to his touch, and her skin was clammy. Her breath was coming in short bursts, and she was still wearing her damp clothes. She was going into shock.

He tightened his arms around her and gently stroked her hair.

'Try to slow your breathing,' he whispered.

He had taken away her choice by seizing the Time Weaver. Was it the right thing to do? Would she forgive him?

'Raf, get some water for her, some food?'

He took off his jacket and wrapped it around Essie's shoulders, pulling her back against his chest.

'You're safe. Nothing is going to happen to you. I am here.'

A few minutes passed as he rocked her. Her shivering body slowly stilled. As her breathing settled, she sat up, moving back from him a little. Blinking, she wiped at her eyes.

Her father was still on the couch, his face blank. How much of what just happened did he understand? Would he ever be the man he was again?

Astari was suddenly in the doorway. She was still, her dark eyes watchful.

He stood up, pulling Essie to her feet.

'I am sorry, Doctor Essie, for your loss,' she said quietly.

Essie shook her head, dabbing at her eyes and nose. 'I am sorry – for Dharma, for everything.'

Astari moved towards her, her long hair swaying. She took Essie's hand.

'Do not blame yourself. This is not your fault.'

Essie ducked her head.

Astari glanced at David, and he cleared his throat. 'We have to move Dharma's body and leave here. Somehow Anna, the Bloodborn, found Essie and her father on a country road, in the middle of nowhere. It stands to reason that they know where we are and it's not safe for us to stay anymore.'

'We must burn Dharma's body, in the tradition.'

He nodded his agreement. All Amaranthine and Bloodborn bodies were disposed of this way, to guard their secret. Even a drop of blood from a dead Amaranthine could reveal them to the human world. This was not the time to get sloppy with such details. Astari's gaze flitted back to Essie, and he noticed she'd gone pale. She was still at risk of shock. He pulled her closer and put his arm around her.

Raf brought her a glass of water and a biscuit.

'Here,' he said, handing the glass to her. She took it and went to her father, helping him to take a few sips. Once he had done so, she wiped her sleeve across the rim of the glass and sipped from it herself. She took the biscuit and nibbled on it. Slowly, the colour started returning to her cheeks. He turned to Raf.

'There was an incinerator here, remember? That factory on the edge of Mount Major?'

Raf's face tightened in horror.

'What are we, barbarians? Dharma was warrior, in the tradition of Amaranthine. He will have warrior's funeral.'

He shook his head.

'We can't light a funeral pyre here, Raf. The Bloodborns are still out there, not to mention humans . . . we can't risk it.'

'I know place,' Raf said, holding up his hand in a way that did not invite any further conversation. 'We go.'

David glanced at Astari. She nodded her ascent.

'All right.'

ASTARI HAD WASHED Dharma's body and wrapped him in a clean sheet. David winced as he lowered him into the boot of the car. In the end, for all his youthful bluster, he had given his life to protect Essie and her father. There was no more he could have asked of him. Now he regretted his antagonism and ill feeling. He wished he had more of an opportunity to get to know him.

Raf took the steering wheel, and he sat beside him. Astari, Essie, and Gilbert sat abreast across the back, packed in tightly. Essie hadn't spoken much since her breakdown at the house, but she had eaten a little more and seemed calmer. Her eyes had lost the crazed look from earlier, and her heart rate had returned to normal. As they drove off, Astari stared out the window, her face placid and her eyes dry. Despite everything that had happened, and her unimaginable heartbreak, she radiated a kind of peace. Gilbert murmured to himself on and off, becoming quite animated at times. He couldn't make out much of what he was saying. It seemed to be largely gibberish. When he became agitated, Essie took his busy hands and held them in her lap.

Raf drove them back onto the highway, in the opposite direction of Ridgeway Lane. After twenty minutes or so, he turned the car down an unmarked dirt road and followed it for five or six kilometres until the end of the track. He pulled over, the tyres crunching on the gravel.

'Where are we?' David asked, squinting through the windscreen.

'I don't know. It is place I came sometimes. When we lived around here. There is path that leads into valley. Cannot see it from road.'

David sighed and rubbed the palms of his hands over his eyes. Funerals were always difficult. But he had only ever heard about Amaranthine funerals from Raf. Looking out into the darkness surrounding them, visions of his dreams, of the multitude of dead Amaranthine, swelled up again. Was it possible that Astari was right? Could Enki still be alive? If so, why would he appear here and now, of all times and places? The answer danced in his subconscious, somewhere just out of reach. He hoped it would come to him in time to prevent any more bloodshed.

'Coming?' Raf asked.

David tensed and opened the car door.

Chapter 20

Essie

Flames licked at the night sky, bright and hot. Essie sat a good distance from the fire, perched on a rocky outcrop. The eucalyptus trees stretched their branches towards the endless canopy, like ghostly limbs encircling the little clearing where the vampires had placed fallen logs in a funeral pyre. The air was heavy with smoke and sorrow. The pain and grief that had crippled her earlier was more subdued now, a dull ache. But the mottled skin between her thumb and index finger tingled. When goosebumps rose on her arms, she pulled the folds of David's jacket around her. For over twenty years, she had almost never cried about her mother or her father. But now she tasted saltiness as tear tracks made their way down her cheeks and she made no effort to conceal them.

Her father sat a little apart from her, hugging himself. He still seemed lost in the wilderness of his mind. She'd tried to pick out individual words or ideas from what he said, but it was mostly garbled nonsense.. His mouth was set in a dull curve, his eyes troubled. Had she lost him forever? Or was there some way to reverse what had happened to him? Although she had known him for her whole life, after what she had done, a part of her felt like she was seeing him for the first time. Before, she had never understood how he could have betrayed her. Allying with Sabine and the Bloodborns. Stealing her work on Zion's Loop. But all her certainty about his culpability had evaporated in the face of her own failings.

'Are you all right?' David touched her elbow, drawing her out of her thoughts. She nodded mechanically.

'I think there might be another clean handkerchief in that pocket of my jacket.' He pointed to it. She gave a half-smile at their little joke. She should start carrying her own handkerchiefs. She seemed to use them more often than he did.

Slipping her hand inside, she retrieved the clean square of fabric, using it to dab at her wet cheeks.

'Do you want this back? You must be cold.' She shrugged the jacket down her arms.

A sad smile crossed his face.

'You keep it.' He pulled it back over her shoulders, his hands resting on the lapels as he stared into her eyes. 'I don't feel the cold. Not like you.'

She held his gaze for a moment before turning away. She was vaguely aware that Rafael was standing across the other side of the clearing beside Astari. But she kept her eyes fixed on the flames. She could not look directly at Astari, could not contemplate her loss. What was she going to do now without Dharma? The existence of the

Amaranthine seemed lonely enough when they had a pair for company. Astari said she had waited a long time after the death of her maker to sire Dharma, and now he was gone. There would be no more chances for her. The thought of immortality with no peer, without anyone to mark the long years with, or share the secret of their existence, seemed like a crushing weight to bear.

But at least Astari still had purpose. The ancient vow of all Amaranthine was to protect the human race. What did she have now? A dead mother and a father gone out of his mind. The idea of her work no longer propelled her. New discoveries, striving at academic endeavour, had once sparked excitement. But now, all of that seemed covered in a pall of blackness. It was her curiosity that had led them down this path, to this very moment. Who was she to think she could ever have sought to manipulate such a powerful force as time? Had she learnt nothing from Sabine? Her future self must not have experienced any of this. Or had she? Where did the past end and the present begin? And was the future still in sight, or was it being changed right now by her actions? What was it that Einstein had said?

The separation between past, present, and future is only an illusion.

A part of her longed for the illusion to be restored to her, for time to be a straight and immutable line. Dependable. Indestructible. Only moving forwards.

A voice sounded in the darkness, clear and light. Astari was singing again. Essie didn't know the song and the words were in another language, yet it was as if she had always heard the tune, somewhere in her heart. Rich tenor notes joined in, humming along with the melody. The flames illuminated David's skin, dancing in the light of his azure eyes while he sang. She closed her eyes as the cadence of the music washed over. In her mind, she pictured Dharma, healthy and whole, as he had been when they met, only a day ago. He gave her a cheeky grin and flicked cigarette ash on the ground. More tears leaked from her eyes, a seemingly endless flood. The song ended, and only the crackle of the flames remained. She felt warmth as an arm extended around her shoulder. She leaned into David's side.

His breath whispered against her hair. 'I won't let anything happen to you, or your father. I'll get you safely home.'

She nodded again, but without feeling. It wasn't that she didn't believe him. She knew that he meant it and that he was capable of it. He could protect her from most physical threats – vampire and human. And he'd already shown that he would. But no one, not even him, could protect her from this. From grief. From loss. From emotion. From the overwhelming swell of it, lodging in her heart again.

'What will she do now?'

'Astari?' He hesitated. 'I don't know.'

'We could take her back with us?'

He didn't answer her. Even as the words left her mouth, she knew it wasn't possible. It wasn't one of the rules they'd been given, but she had a strong sense that removing someone out of their natural timeline and taking them to the future could have untold ramifications. She swallowed and wiped at the tears on her face with the handkerchief again.

'I'm sorry.' She sniffed. 'I messed up. I knew it was wrong to do what I did, but I did it anyway.'

His arm squeezed tighter around her shoulder.

'I understand,' he murmured. 'It's all right.'

She bowed her head.

'It's not all right. I acted so irrationally. I couldn't comprehend why my father did what he did – helping Sabine. I thought it was unforgivable. But now . . .'

He was silent for a long moment. She tensed, bracing herself for his reaction. But he reached down and threaded his fingers through hers. There was a warmth and a comfort in his presence, even though she didn't deserve his compassion.

'Reason is your bastion, and there's nothing wrong with that. But reason will only get you so far, Essie. In matters of the heart, logic is like a compass. It can point us in the right direction, but it never guarantees us safe passage.'

'What guarantee is there then?' She tried to keep the edge of frustration from her voice. 'How can we keep ourselves safe from *this*?'

Before he could answer, the air shifted, and Rafael appeared by his side.

'It is done, *Dado*. We scatter ashes and find Bloodborns. Then we leave this time.'

David squeezed her hand briefly before releasing her.

'We'll drop you to a motel. I want you both to wait

there while we hunt the Bloodborns. I'll ask Astari to stay with you.'

She opened her mouth to protest. She wanted to stay with him. But Rafael glared at her. And she wasn't in any position to complain. Not after everything that had happened, after what she had done. So, she turned to her father and helped him to his feet.

As they walked back to the car arm in arm, she glanced over her shoulder. Astari stood in the darkness, her slender finger silhouetted against the dying flames. She pressed two fingers to her lips before reaching out and touching them to the smouldering, ashen pile of wood. Her gaze drifted to the starry sky, then she bent to spread the embers.

Chapter 21

David

David inserted the worn key and the motel door creaked open. The room was as tired looking as the one in Feldham that Rhonda had rented them two nights before. It too had smelt damp and uninviting. But they couldn't return to the house. This was safer.

Essie followed him through the door. She settled Gilbert on the edge of the bed.

'Why don't you have a lie down, Dad? It must have been a while since you had a proper sleep. Sun still won't be up for a little while.'

She knelt in front of him and removed his shoes. He swung his legs onto the bed without protest. His lips moved with whispered words, like a meditation. He folded his hands under his chin and closed his eyes.

Raf and Astari waited outside the room, their eyes scanning the horizon in vigilance as they discussed plans for the next steps. So far, there had been no more signs of the Bloodborns. They would have to hunt them down somehow.

David half-closed the motel door and drew Essie aside.

'Promise me you'll stay here with Astari until I get back.'

He searched her face for a sign of acquiescence. All he could see was the pain and regret in her eyes. She was still punishing herself for what she had done.

'I promise,' she said at last.

'We've only got a few hours until dawn. But we'll keep searching until we find them. When we return, you and Gilbert must be ready to leave. Immediately.'

'We'll be ready.'

She unbuttoned his suit jacket and shrugged it off, handing it to him.

'I know you don't feel the cold, but you can't go hunting Bloodborns without this. You don't look like yourself. I'm keeping the handkerchief though.' She stuffed the folded cloth into her own pocket.

He flashed her a half-smile as he slipped his arms back through his jacket sleeves. Her fragrance clung to the fabric. The suit would always be marked by her scent now. A permanent reminder of her presence in his life. As if he needed any such tokens. She had already left an immovable mark on his heart. He straightened the jacket and adjusted his tie.

'Does that look better, then?'

She appraised him and nodded her approval.

'Astari will be here, just in case there's any trouble. We'll be back as soon as possible.'

'What will you do when you find them?'

His heart clenched. How much more death could she handle right now? And yet, there was no other way. Bloodborns were beyond any hope of redemption. And she knew what his vow was, the reason for his very existence.

'They're young vampires. Poorly trained. It should be quick. Merciful.'

She nodded.

'Be careful though. Don't let them infect you . . . make sure you . . . I don't know.'

She rambled, her words all a jumble. Touching her shoulder gently, he smiled.

'I'll be careful.'

He turned to leave, but as he did, she caught his hand in hers. She'd done it a few times before – touched him of her own accord. But it still brought him up short. Not just because it had been such a long time since any human had touched him intentionally other than a formal shake of hands. It was also the feel of her skin on his, her warm fragility. His traitorous heart raced in response, no matter how he tried to ignore it. He shouldn't want this. Want her. Raf and Astari were right outside the door.

And yet . . .

He turned and leaned towards her. His fingertips whispered along her cheekbone as he tucked a strand of her wayward hair behind her ear. Lingering for a moment, his face was so close to hers. Her breaths were shallow. The blood rushing through her veins answered his own. He smiled at the knowledge.

'I'll see you soon.'

He softly pressed her hand, then stepped out into the night, closing the door behind him.

Raf cleared his throat, throwing him a dark look he chose to ignore.

Astari drew out a thin object from her jacket and handed it to Raf. Dharma's sword. 'You may as well have use of this now.'

Raf unsheathed it and turned it over. The metal glinted under the fluorescent lighting of the motel balcony. It was shorter and lighter than David's broadsword, but it looked sharp and manoeuvrable. And they didn't have any other such weapons. It would be useful.

'Thank you,' Raf said, sheathing the blade again and tucking it under his arm. 'We go, *Dado*.'

He turned to Astari and opened his mouth to speak, but she silenced him with a raised hand.

'I know what you will say, but there is no need. I will keep them safe.'

David nodded, grateful. Astari disappeared inside the room, closing the door behind her.

THEY DROVE the streets of Mount Major in silence. Although tracking the Bloodborns on foot would be easier, if they needed to dispose of bodies, the car would be handy for concealing and transporting them once the sun was up. Raf's face was expressionless, his hands resting on the wheel. He seemed to be deliberately avoiding David's gaze, keeping his eyes firmly fixed on the road.

'You can just say it, Raf.'

'There is nothing I am saying.'

'Are you sure? I know you heard us at the motel. No warnings about getting involved with humans? No advice on maintaining distance and self-control?'

He shrugged and changed his grip on the steering wheel.

'I am not your keeper or your conscience. You are grown man. You make own choices.'

He sighed. He hated disappointing Raf. And he didn't want to fight with him. But this was different. She was different.

'I will only say, *Dado*, that what I have taught you about keeping distance is not only for your benefit. You are selfless, kind. You give anything, sacrifice anything, for her. But have you thought – what will she give up for you, to be with you? Is that weight you can bear?'

He turned his face to the window, watching the streetlights pass. They were two species never meant to mix. Like water and oil. And yet not quite. All immortals were human once. A seed must fall to the ground and die to be reborn a flower. So the coil of mortality lingered in the Amaranthine. Would he ever be able to shrug it off? More to the point though, he didn't even know if she wanted that with him. A future. Her lifetime.

'I don't know how she feels about me. She's a rationalist . . . a scientist. It dictates her whole outlook . . .'

Even as the words were leaving his mouth, he tasted the lie behind them and stopped. He remembered what she had been through, how she had responded – not with logic but with pure feeling. And he remembered her response to him, the blood pulsing under his touch as he said goodbye.

A charged silence fell in the car. Raf turned off onto a poorly lit road that climbed gradually towards a summit. The titular mountain of the town of Mount Major. They passed a sign for the Knots Pine Cemetery. Pulling into a large, empty parking lot at the back of the cemetery, Raf killed the engine.

'A cemetery? It's a bit cliché, don't you think?'

He huffed.

'Maybe, but has good view.' He indicated the town below, dotted with streetlights and moving cars. 'And helps me think. Put pieces of puzzle together.'

David nodded slowly. There were lots of pieces, and though he sensed they had to be connected somehow, he was still struggling to work it out.

'The Bloodborns tracked Essie to the park outside the library because she had the Time Weaver. It wasn't an ideal time or location, but it was strategic and planned. They had a specific target. When that failed, Anna hunted Essie down on an isolated country road in the middle of nowhere, at exactly the right time.'

Raf twirled one end of his moustache between his fingers.

'There is also bloodrot, *Dado*. No Bloodborn under a century would carry this infection. The disease has died out.'

'Perhaps Sabine was a carrier? It was her blood that turned Anna and Jono. She could have passed it on to them.'

Raf shook his head. 'From what Nika explain, it must be direct contact to pass the infection.'

'All right. What are you thinking then?'

Raf flicked on the radio. The local station disc jockey broke into the closing lines of a song, announcing the next day's weather prediction and upcoming football games. Normal small town chatter. Nothing more interesting or out of the ordinary. David made the mental leap, and suddenly knew exactly what Raf would say next.

'The Bloodborns should be hungry, starving. Newborns are opportunistic feeders, especially without anyone to rein them in.'

The older vampire gave a slight nod of his head, a lock of his silver curls falling across his forehead.

David continued. 'Sabine did not have time to train them in the art of clandestine feeding. When Essie arrived in the church, Sabine was barely able to control their blood lust. Like gutter rats, once they landed here, they would normally feed on the first thing they could find.'

He glanced out the window. The cemetery loomed in the distance. An excavating machine, presumably used to dig the graves, lay idle by the front gate.

'They be here at least three days now. If they act alone, there should be more bodies. More missing. At least an attack. But I check at police station, I check TV, radio. Nothing. So where they feeding?'

Some of the pieces clicked together in David's mind. Raf hadn't driven them up to the cemetery just for the view.

'They've been feeding in the graveyard.'

He smiled wryly.

'Have seen before. There is reason for stories about vampires and graveyards. The dead don't complain. But still does not explain attack in park. Someone helped them. But why? Bloodborns don't play well together.'

'Why do they do anything, Raf? You've said it yourself. They exist to cause chaos and destruction.'

'Mmm, perhaps . . .' He frowned, tilting his head.

A disturbance rippled the atmosphere around them, shaking the car's frame. David tensed and Raf's hand went to Dharma's sword automatically. A movement in the darkness caught his eyes. Shadows flitted through the trees. They were fast and light, moving too quickly for human eyes to track. And they carried the scent of death on them.

Chapter 22

Essie

E ssie pulled her legs up onto the bed and crossed them in front of her. Her father was snoring softly, which was a relief. He had to be exhausted after everything that had happened. She was certainly exhausted. In her bones. In her muscles. In every sinew barely holding her together now. Yet she knew she would not sleep. How could she? Her hand fidgeted with the dried wound on her neck before clasping around the bicycle pendant.

Please protect David. And Rafael too.

She felt David's absence like she had felt the change in temperature when she gave him back his suit jacket. The warm blanket of his presence had left with him. Now the dark seemed frightening and unknown. His words at the funeral pyre came back to her, and she turned them over in her mind.

Logic is like a compass.

It can point us in the right direction, but it never guarantees us safe passage.

'Shall I make you some tea, Doctor Essie? David also said you should have some more to eat.'

She snorted. Maybe David's presence wasn't completely gone. It was very like him to take every opportunity to make her eat and drink. Sometimes she felt like a prize goose he was trying to fatten up. But a cup of tea didn't sound like the worst idea.

'Please just call me Essie, and I'd love some tea, thank you.'

Astari plugged a little kettle into the power socket, and minutes later, the bubbling noise signalled the water was boiling. She placed tea bags into two cups and poured the hot water over them. Even doing something so simple, her every movement was fluid and graceful, her sheer jacket floating around her. She took a little jug of milk from the fridge and added some to one of the cups before handing it to her.

'You Australians like milk, I think?'

'I do.' She took it gratefully. 'Is there any sugar?'

Astari fished around the tray of tea things and retrieved two sachets of sugar, handing them to her. Essie ripped them open and dumped the contents of both into the cup.

'You like it sweet, huh? In Southeast Asia, where I am from, we also like our tea sweet. Except we usually drink it cold. It's too humid for hot drinks most of the time.'

It didn't take much imagination for her to picture Astari in a warmer climate, sipping iced tea in the heat. In her mind, she saw Dharma there too. Then the picture flashed to him with his fangs bared, his face distorted. She tried to suppress a shudder.

'I think you are cold though, Doctor Essie. You should drink your tea. It will warm you up.'

She blew across the surface of the cup before taking a tentative sip. The steam fogged her glasses a little as the warm, sweet liquid slid down the back of her throat. It tasted good. But she found her mind drifting back to David. Astari settled herself in the only chair in the room.

'You are worried about them. It is not an irrational fear. But I think they are very experienced. And your David is fast.'

She huffed, her cheeks heating up.

'He's not *mine*. We're just . . . we're friends.'

As she said the words, she knew it wasn't true anymore. She thought about how he had caressed her cheek, his face so close to hers. His eyes mesmerising. When he leaned in, she had thought he might kiss her. His scent washed over her, warm and inviting. What would it be like to kiss him?

But he had also told her before, in no uncertain terms, that relationships between vampires and humans were a bad idea. She could see why. All his reasons made sense. And why would she set herself up for more pain? The past few days had brought enough of that. It had almost killed her. What if she opened her heart to him and he broke it too? Cecil had urged her not to be an island anymore, but it was too hard. She didn't know how to not be alone.

'I understand, you know,' Astari said at last. 'I have loved people I should not have. I married two of them.'

'Married?' Essie sputtered her tea.

Astari laughed lightly. 'Yes. Both human. Before I made Dharma.'

'But what happened to them?'

'They died, just like we all do in the end. Even vampires are not truly immortal.'

'I'm sorry. That must have been difficult. When they died.'

Her gaze dropped to the floor. She plucked at the lace on her sleeve.

'Painful, yes. But sometimes not in the way you might expect. The real pain was realising someone I thought I could trust had betrayed me.'

Something in Astari's tone kept Essie from asking who had done that to her. She glanced at her father. She knew betrayal all too well. Her feelings about him were more complicated now though. Now that she had been the one to betray all of them. She wasn't sure how she would sort through the mess of her emotions. It would take time.

The silence dragged on as she tried to think of a new topic of conversation, something that was safer ground. Her mind turned to David again, to the dreams he had mentioned.

'Astari, do you really believe all those stories about your origins, about the god who created the Bloodborns?'

She tilted her head to the side slightly, a small furrow forming across her brow as she shrugged.

'Enki? Hmmm. Perhaps.'

'Have you ever seen anything to make you believe it's real? The Amaranthine are phenomenal. The Bloodborns are too, from a scientific perspective. But I also think that science can explain any phenomenon. Sometimes it just takes a while to figure it out.'

A smile ghosted across Astari's lips and she took a sip of her tea.

'Every culture has its origin stories. Greek and Norse mythology, the Aztecs. I used to love those stories when I was a kid. But then I grew up, and I learnt that humans made up those stories to explain the things that they didn't understand. Alchemy, weather patterns, the flat earth. Science explained it all. The truth is there are no gods and monsters.'

Astari gave a short laugh. 'Maybe there are no real gods, but there are certainly monsters in this world, Doctor Essie. The difficulty is that monsters sometimes seem like angels. The hero can sometimes be a villain in disguise.'

Her dark eyes were intent, her stare fixed on Essie. She shifted uncomfortably.

'Essie!' She jumped, her tea splashing out of the cup.

Her father bolted upright, shouting. He reached his hands out in front of him, trying to grasp some unseen force. She placed her teacup down and went over to him.

'It's okay, Dad. You were just having a nightmare.'

She tried to take his outstretched hands in hers to calm him, but he reefed himself free. Swinging his legs onto the floor, he ran barefoot towards the door, his fingers fumbling at the lock.

'We have to go . . .'

When he failed to get the lock undone, he started banging his fist on the door.

'Let us out! Let us out!'

'Dad, calm down. It was just a dream.'

She tried to drag him away from the door. Where was Astari? Why wasn't she helping? Her father swung his arms about wildly and she ducked, narrowly missing being struck by his fist.

'Dad, stop! You're going to hurt me.'

He turned his face to her. Her stomach clenched. He was barely recognisable. The dull, faraway look in his eyes had been replaced with a steely menace. She took two quick steps backwards.

'Dad . . .'

He pivoted around, grabbing for the door handle again. She lunged at him, but he wrenched the door open in the same moment, smacking her straight in the face. The sharp edge hit her forehead and sent a crack of pain reverberating through her body. She fell backwards, landing hard. Reaching for her throbbing brow, her fingertips found sticky wetness. As she tried to focus her blurry vision, she sensed someone leaning over her, dark hair falling over their shoulder as they smiled. Then everything swirled around her, and her eyes slid closed as blackness claimed her.

Chapter 23

David

Raf turned to David, his eyes alert but calm. He flourished Dharma's sword and tossed the sheath onto the back seat of the car in one languid movement.

'They are here.'

He opened the car door, and the night air rushed in. David put his hand on Raf's arm.

'We can't kill them yet. If there's another Bloodborn here, helping them, we need to find out who and where they are hiding.'

There was a loud thud overhead. An arm flopped onto the windscreen like a discarded doll. The hand was covered in red, as though it had been dipped in paint. But the metallic tang of blood hit the back of his throat with a rush.

Damn it. Human.

It took him a second to leap onto the roof of the car. The man's head lolled to the side, eyes open and vacant. David listened for a heartbeat, but there was only silence.

'Dado!'

There was no time to react. Anna's attack came with more stealth than he had anticipated. She landed on top of the car with lightning swiftness, fangs bared, and eyes burning crimson. A small, golden blade glinted in her hand and his stomach reeled. She stabbed at him, and he responded reflexively, knocking it from her hand as he delivered a blow to her arm with his boot. She reacted as quickly, latching onto his arm. She wrenched his cuff open, the button popping off.

'Where is it?'

She tore at his arm in a frenzy, her fingernails opening grooves down his skin. He twisted his body, pulling his arm free and countering with another kick. She flew backwards, landing in dense scrub. He pivoted, scanning for Raf and Jono, but there was no sight of them.

He launched himself down from the roof of the car onto Anna's prone body. She shrieked and slipped out from under him. Flicking his wrist, he caught her ankle as she tried to run. She tumbled over, landing heavily on a stone grave top. He climbed onto her, using all his weight to hold her down. Her free hands clawed for his coat pockets, searching.

'You won't get it.'

He grabbed her wrists and pinned them over her head. She snarled in frustration.

'You're pathetic!' She kept twisting her body as she tried to escape his grip. 'You followed her here like a lovesick puppy.'

'I came here for you and Jono. That's what we do. Hunt Bloodborns. Or didn't Sabine explain that part to you?'

He took his eyes from her briefly, searching for Raf again in the distant trees.

'Sabine was a crappy teacher. There were some key details she left out. Like how a thirst for blood can drive you nearly mad, how it makes your throat feel like someone set a fire in it.'

She shoved her hips upwards, trying to shift his body off her, but he was far heavier. He centred his weight, holding her firmly in place.

'I think you've been feeding quite well lately, if that poor man's anything to go by.' He jerked his head towards the corpse on top of the car.

Anna licked her bloodstained lips, her eyes glinting.

'It's not the same as drinking from the living, but anything is better than starving. And they deliver them to us here, almost every day.'

Raf reappeared next to the car. He had Jono in a secure hold in front of him, Dharma's blade resting on his throat. David exhaled with relief.

'This is over now, Anna. Rafael will kill Jono. Then I will kill you.'

She threw a careless glance in Jono's direction.

'Do whatever you like to him. He's more annoying now than he ever was as my human boyfriend.'

Jono growled, struggling to free himself of Raf's grip.

'You've stayed undetected, feeding in the cemetery. But you can't be hiding out here in the daytime. Who told you about the Time Weaver? How did you trace Essie to the library and Ridgeway Lane?'

She smirked, her red eyes darting to Raf, then back to him.

Raf pushed Jono forwards until he was level with Anna's head. He lowered the sword from Jono's neck and touched the tip to Anna's throat. 'Tell us!'

She shrank from the blade but pressed her lips together firmly.

'When we went through that wormhole, everything was a blur.'

David looked up at Jono as he spoke. Anna scowled at him, but he swallowed and went on.

'We woke up here, alone. But she found us. She said if we helped her get the Time Weaver, she could take us home.'

'What do you mean? She *who*?'

'Your girlfriend hasn't figured it out yet?' Anna gave a short laugh and the movement caused the tip of the sword to pierce her skin. She hissed.

'Typical. She always thought she was so smart, but she can never see what's right in front of her nose.'

David's eyes met Raf's, searching for the answer. Had the older vampire been right all along? Was Rhonda really not who she seemed to be? Had she betrayed them? But now she was also dead, wasn't she?

Anna kicked against him again, striking his shin. He stretched her arms higher over her head and brought his knee up into her chest. She yelped.

'Where have you been hiding? Who's protecting you?'

He shook her roughly and smacked her head against the stone beneath them. Her lips curled into a pained sneer.

'Why should I tell you? You're just going to kill me anyway! You said yourself, that's what you do.' She eyed the sword at her throat.

'Enough!' Raf barked. 'This is waste of time. Let's get this over with, *Dado*.'

David stepped back and hauled Anna to her feet. She staggered forwards, and he gripped her by the shoulders, forcing her upright. Her stained shirt caught his eye. The blood pattern was strange. He leaned in closer. It wasn't just blood. There was an insignia on the pocket. He had seen it somewhere before. The insignia bore a name: Mount Major Secondary School. It was the red and white crest of Essie's high school. But why was Anna wearing a school uniform? Where did she get it? He felt a sudden rush of understanding. It was January. School was out for the summer holidays. It had been out since Christmas. The building would be basically deserted for a few more weeks.

'They've been hiding out at the high school,' he said to Rafael, pointing at Anna's shirt. 'That's the school's crest. Essie pointed it out to us when we arrived, remember?'

Raf frowned, then tilted his head.

'Wow.' Anna smirked. 'Look who turned out to be the genius, after all. Shame you can't use the Time Weaver yourself. I guess she didn't trust you with it.'

You can't use it yourself.

The Bloodborns had followed them to the cemetery to

get the bracelet. They knew he had it. Anna's words to Essie at Ridgeway Lane came back to him.

I'm not allowed to kill you yet.

Why? Because they also seemed to know the Time Weaver was useless without Essie, which meant whoever was helping them knew that too.

Essie.

His jaw clenched.

'Whoever sent these two knows they need Essie for the Time Weaver to work.'

Anna snickered.

'Ding, ding, ding! Ten points to you,' she deadpanned.

Raf growled at her, inching the blade closer to her neck. Her crimson eyes stared back at him defiantly. She pulled her lips back, revealing her elongated incisors.

They need Essie.

'We have to get back to the motel. Now!'

Chapter 24

Essie

Essie struggled to open her eyes as consciousness came back to her. She blinked a few times and squinted. Pain seared down the side of her head. She tried to lift her hand to touch it, but her arms were bound. She was tied to a chair. A cold draught blew from somewhere, scattering goosebumps over her skin.

'Astari?' she whispered. She cleared her throat and tried again more loudly. 'Astari?'

No answer. Fear settled over her. Where was she? What had happened? Where was Astari? And where was her father?

'Dad?'

Again, no response. Just her voice, echoing in the silence.

Breathe, Essie.

Just breathe.

David will be here soon.

She closed her eyes and tried to stay calm.

'I know he will come for me.'

Laughter echoed around her. Mocking. Sinister.

'I'm counting on it, Doctor Essie.'

Chapter 25

David

'We're too late!'

He slammed the motel door so hard the handle dislodged and toppled to the ground. Raf grunted as he sat down on the bed.

'What if a powerful Bloodborn took them, like Sabine? Or maybe Enki is still alive after all? Whoever they are, they must be old if they were able to supply Anna and Jono with a bloodrot-infected blade.'

Raf held the golden sword that Anna had brought to the cemetery to the light, inspecting it.

'This is same blade she use on Dharma.' He carefully sheathed it again.

They had used it to dispose of Anna and Jono by the only means certain to kill a Bloodborn. Then they were forced to waste precious minutes returning the human corpse to his gravesite and carefully digging up another one to bury the Bloodborns. They couldn't burn the bodies. A fire on the top of a hill would draw too much attention, especially as dawn approached. So they found an older grave, one whose occupant was unlikely to be visited by relatives now, and tossed them in. The nice thing about traditional gravestones was once you placed the cement slab back over the hole, it was difficult to tell that anything had been disturbed. Hopefully, no one would dig it up again. At least not for a long time.

But David's mind raced with the million worst possibilities about what had happened to Essie. And her father. And Astari. His breaths came in short bursts as he paced the room.

'They will not hurt her, *Dado*. They are after Time Weaver so they need her. And was not Bloodborns. Use your senses. They have not been here.'

He paused, sniffed the air. Of course. If Bloodborns had been in the room, it would reek of their scent. Thank God Raf was still thinking clearly.

'We go to school. That is where Bloodborns were hiding.'

They began walking back towards the car. Raf hesitated, then stumbled and keened to the side.

'What's wrong?' David reached out an arm to steady him.

'Is nothing.' Raf brushed off his hand. 'My knee sore from chasing Bloodborn. It goes away soon. *Andiamo*'

David frowned, unconvinced. Clearly, all the recent fighting was taking its toll on Raf. They had no more supplies of blood and there was no time to stop and worry about it now. At least the headaches had not returned for

him. He felt strong. They'd have to worry about Raf's
health later.

HE PULLED the car up at the high school and killed the
engine just as dawn broke. The building was silent. The
windows across the façade were tightly shut, blinds
drawn. He went to the iron gates and shook the heavy,
padlocked chain. It rattled securely in place. All locked up.
But that didn't mean anything. It wasn't the type of
countermeasure that would keep vampires out.

Raf threw Dharma's sword and the golden knife over
the gate. He launched himself up next, perching atop the
barrier for a split second before dipping deftly down the
other side, the flaps of his leather coat flying out like wings.
David followed and landed beside him. They darted across
the driveway and edged along the side of the building.
Halfway along, he noticed a set of double wooden doors. He
stopped and looked at Raf, wordlessly asking if this was a
good entry point. Raf gave a slight nod of his head in
agreement. David tried the handle. When it didn't give way,
he braced himself and threw his shoulder into it. The wood
splintered, the lock falling away as the doors swung open.

A voice pierced the air from overhead. Female.
Frightened.

Essie.

He was sprinting towards the cry before he even
realised his legs were moving. He rounded a corner and

flew up a set of stairs, coming into a long, windowless corridor. Essie's cry was getting louder. He was close. She had to be behind one of the doors coming off the corridor.

A strong hand grabbed his arm, halting his pace.

'Wait, *Dado*.' Raf's voice was a low whisper. He stood in front of him, a hand pressed to his chest.

'This is obviously trap, and she is the – how do you say – like fishing?'

'Bait,' David finished.

'Yes, bait.' He nodded. 'Whoever help Bloodborns, they lure us here also. We must have plan.'

He wanted to keep running, to find Essie, but Raf's dark eyes pinned him. He clenched his hand into a tight ball with the effort of holding himself back.

'We have to get her out of there, Raf.'

'We will. You go first, carefully. I circle round and find other entrance. Then I make diversion. It will be loud noise. Understand?'

He nodded, and Raf released his arm. It was the smarter approach.

'Give me bracelet. I hide it. Keep it safe.'

Another good idea. Keep Essie and the Time Weaver separate. He reached into his waistcoat and handed it over. Raf carefully tucked the golden knife into his belt and pocketed the Time Weaver before ghosting away down the corridor. David crept forwards, edging along the wall past two more closed doors. He paused outside a door with large gold lettering over the arch. The library. At last, he caught Essie's scent. But something was wrong. There were sweet cloves and soap somewhere in the mix, but it was almost overpowered by the scent of death. The pall of it hung about her like dried roses. His lungs contracted inwards.

No.

No.

He was too late. His breath left his lungs. Then he heard it.

Thump-thump.

The steady beat of her human heart. He sighed quietly, shoulders relaxing. She was still alive.

As soundlessly as he could, he nudged the library door open. She was in the middle of the room, trussed up to a chair. Shelves of books surrounded her on all sides, lining the library walls. He mouth was gagged, head hanging to her chest. Her hands were tied behind her back. She shivered and a wave of guilt swept over him. This was all his fault. It seemed no matter how hard he tried, she always ended up in danger.

A loud bang came from the corridor. Raf's distraction. That was his cue. In the next breath, he sped silently to Essie's side. She inhaled sharply as he laid his hand gently on her shoulder.

'It's all right, it's me.' He reached for the ropes around her wrist and untied them with a single twist.

He pulled the filthy rag from around her mouth. As he tore it free, he noticed the blood. Dried blood on her chin, her neck. He looked her over. She appeared unharmed. Had the wound on her neck re-opened? Where had all the blood come from?

'Are you hurt?'

She shook her head.

'Someone's here.' She mouthed. 'I could hear them!'

'We found Anna and Jono. They've had help from the beginning. That's how they knew about the Time Weaver, how to find you – twice. Whoever it is, they brought you here.'

'What about Dad and Astari? I don't know where they are.'

Her voice was panicked, fearful. He took her by the hand.

'Follow me. We're going to get you out of here. Then we'll find them.'

The overhead lights blasted on, one fluorescent tube at a time, illuminating the bookshelves in their wake. Essie flinched, shielding her eyes with her hands. He pulled her against his side and started moving towards the door.

A slender shape with long, dark hair slipped out from behind one of the bookshelves. He raised his eyebrows.

'Where have you been?'

Astari's mouth curled into a smile, revealing razor-sharp teeth. She inclined her head at Essie. 'She'll be the death of you, you know.'

He wavered for a moment, disbelieving. Then all the pieces clicked together and acceptance swept over him. He tensed.

Astari held a small blade aloft, pointing it towards Essie. It was the golden knife. The one Raf had tucked into his belt earlier. How did Astari have it now? Fear uncoiled inside him, spreading slowly. Astari shot a glare at him, and he flinched. The pressure in his head struck like a hammer blow.

Not now.

Please not now.

'Astari,' Essie whispered, moving towards her. 'We think there's another Bloodborn here. They've been helping –'

Pushing aside the pain, David yanked her backwards and angled himself in front of her, stretching his arms out to cage her behind him.

Astari took sideways steps, circling them at a distance. She raised the knife vertical to her body and held the tip between her thumb and forefinger. Her eyes were dark crimson, focussed. Essie drew a shocked breath.

'Astari?' Her voice was strangled, incredulous, as she frowned at the knife.

The dark-haired vampire inclined her head.

A succession of disjointed thoughts surged through his mind as he tried to make sense of the deception. His jaw tightened.

'You've been helping them this whole time, haven't you?'

She twirled the little blade in her hand lazily.

'I've been helping them, or they've been helping me. It amounts to the same thing, I suppose.'

'But why, Astari?'

He could hear the tremor in Essie's voice, the doubt. She tried to step past him, and he gripped her arm in warning. He could sense her fear. He was afraid too. Astari hadn't been reverting as long as Raf. She was also completely unpredictable. Not Bloodborn and seemingly not Amaranthine either. He had no idea what she would do next.

She flipped the knife over, catching it by the hilt.

'You can't possibly understand.'

'Try me!' Essie challenged. 'If you're going to betray us, we at least deserve to know why.'

'You *deserve* death,' she hissed, edging forwards. 'But since I still need you.'

She shifted her stance and lowered the knife with a heavy sigh.

'It's a simple tale really. Cliched. Imagine that you love someone so much that you would be willing to die for them. They are mortal. But you are willing to give up your immortal existence so you can be with them in death.'

She stopped and turned her eyes pointedly towards him. The pain in his head flared again, and he fought to stay upright.

'It makes no sense. But their soul speaks to yours in a way that you cannot give voice to. You find a refuge in each other where the world has become so harsh and unfathomable. A silent conversation between two hearts begins, and eventually they beat as one.'

She paused. Moments passed in weighty silence. Her face contorted. The weight of suffering seeped from her pores like oil. Her whole body was tremoring with it. What had happened to her? What had driven her to this point?

'Then imagine that person, your *soul mate*, betrays you. The connection you thought you shared was a cruel lie. Knowing your secret, the secret of what *we* are, they sold you out. Gave you over to be experimented on, tortured, torn apart.'

She pressed her lips together, then let out a bitter laugh.

'Yet we can only die one way. This excites the torturers even more. Imagine the discoveries! What if they could distil the secrets to eternal youth? The possibilities are endless. And so, they rebuild you. And then they start the cruelty all over again.'

Essie exhaled, disgusted.

'You are appalled at my story? My sire always taught me we must protect the humans from the Bloodborns. That is the vow passed down from the elder to the younger. Mortals are innocents, while the Bloodborn, the sons and daughters of chaos, are the monsters. But that's too black and white for this world of shadows, of greyness. Because the Amaranthine ended up forgetting the most important thing. We all came from the same source in the beginning. We were all human once. And that's where the fault lies. It's the humans who are the true monsters. You and your kind are the worst vampires of all.'

Keeping one protective hand on Essie, David took a wobbling step towards Astari, raising his other hand in submission.

'I'm sorry for what you have been through, Astari. But this isn't the way.'

'Ah . . . David. So noble. So just. You defend the humans, though they are utterly worthless. And she is the most worthless of all. The *scientist*. Pretending she will do what is right. But she was like all the rest in the end. She did what served her own selfish interests. And you're just as bad.'

Astari sneered and narrowed her eyes at him. The pain intensified. His headache amplified, his vision blurring. He made the leap in his mind. It was all connected to her. Somehow, she was creating the pressure in his head. And she was the only one who could make it stop.

'What about Dharma? Was he like all the rest?' Essie asked.

Astari's face faltered, anguish colouring her features.

'Oh, my sweet boy.' Tears leaked onto her cheeks. 'After all the long years since my sire's passing, I at last relented. I created another to take my place, so that I could slowly grow old with my human lover and still leave a legacy to follow me. That's when I was betrayed. Dharma helped me escape.'

'And in return, you infected him with bloodrot?'

Her face hardened.

'That was never part of the plan. He was innocent. Anna was meant to infect Rafael, get him out of the picture. But Dharma was like you. Always the hero. And Anna was clumsy. Useless, really.'

She held up the golden blade and flipped a catch on the hilt. It came undone, revealing a small vial filled with red liquid.

'It's a neat little device. It was already filled with the infected blood when I got it. I wasn't even sure it would work.'

David swallowed and backed away. Essie clung to his arm.

'How did you know Anna and Jono were here in the first place?'

Astari flicked the vial closed and laid the sword flat across her palm.

'Now that is a curious thing. I told the truth about my dreams. I saw you in them, and all the dead Amaranthine. I knew it was a sign. I've always read the signs. Then a few weeks ago, this little blade arrived with a note – precise instructions on where to go and when. Anna and Jono were weak when I found them. Surviving on rats and rabbits. It hadn't even occurred to them to feed on the corpses until I showed them. They told me their wild story of wormholes and time travel. And the scientist who was responsible for it all. Then I understood the possibilities.'

She narrowed her crimson eyes at Essie. With a flick of her wrist, the Time Weaver appeared in the palm of her hand. David gasped, fear tightening his stomach. How did she have it? Where was Raf?

Oh God.

'Now it's time to see this thing in action.'

The corners of Astari's mouth lifted into a mocking curve.

Chapter 26

Essie

'What have you done with my father?'

Essie fought to suppress her fear and think clearly. Astari had betrayed them. She had aided Anna and Jono and caused Dharma's death. Now she had the Time Weaver. What if she had hurt her father?

David doubled over in front of her, clutching his head. She tried to help him up.

'What's wrong?'

He cried out and fell to his knees. Astari gave a short laugh, and Essie's eyes flashed to her.

'What's wrong with him? Why is this happening?'

'It's just a little trick. With all the experiments the humans did on me, something changed. Maybe it was evolution? I developed some special abilities. If I concentrate, I can apply pressure to the brain. It's a bit like squeezing a lemon. The effect is different for everyone. Your father, for example. Just after I located the Bloodborns, we found him wandering and alone, so I

200

performed a little test. But it sent him right over the edge. David seems to be more durable, unfortunately. I didn't experiment on you since I needed your brain intact. And doing something to Rafael might have made my little party trick a bit too obvious.'

Essie shook her head as she tried to steady David. He was too heavy for her to lift. She slumped down beside him, her hand on his back. There was an odd taste in her mouth and her lips felt sticky.

'Where is my father? What have you done to him?'

Astari clenched her jaw and narrowed her eyes. David cried out again, tearing desperately at his hair. Essie stroked his back, wishing there was some way she could help him.

'Stop it, please! You're hurting him.'

'*This* is hurting him? Do you have any idea what they did to me? Those human monsters?'

With a shaking hand, Astari pulled the sleeve of her lace jacket up, revealing a jagged, purple scar that stretched from her wrist to her shoulder.

'This is but one of the marks they gave me while they weren't killing me. The Bloodborns are right. Humans are only good for one thing: dying. And without the Amaranthine, that's exactly what will happen to them all.'

'Why are you doing this to us? What do you want?'

'Isn't it obvious? The Time Weaver of course. It must be why I was sent here. Now, my revenge can begin. I will hunt every Amaranthine through history and destroy them one by one. If the humans hadn't created us, their perverted science experiments, none of this would have happened. No one would have resisted the Bloodborns and the horror of this world would not exist.'

David pulled in a breath and raised his head with a visible effort.

'When you get your revenge, will that make you feel better? Will it ease your pain?'

Astari lifted her chin, unmoved by his words.

'Nothing will ever make me *feel* better. But at least if the Amaranthine are gone, then we finally end. It all ends. The futility of this ceaseless war will be over.'

Essie frowned. Nothing was making any sense. Astari wanted to use the Time Weaver to travel in history and get rid of all the Amaranthine who had ever existed. That would include Astari herself.

'If you destroy all of your own kind, you'll be gone too. Then what?'

'Then nothing. The bliss of not feeling. Ever again.'

Astari's eyes were wide, her pupils dilated. Essie had the sensation that she was gazing in a mirror.

Never feel again.

That was something she understood all too well. Only hours earlier, she had wanted the same thing. She would have done anything not to carry that pain. Given anything.

'Astari –'

David tensed. Something moved in the distance, drawing his gaze.

Rafael?

Astari reacted swiftly. With one violent movement, she lifted a row of bookshelves and hurled them across the room. The shelves creaked and buckled as the books tumbled from their places in a rain of paper and bindings. As they crashed to the ground, Essie heard a cry. She squinted. A body protruded from under the shelves.

'Rafael!' His leg was twisted at an awkward angle, the femur partially exposed through his torn pants. Her throat burned with bile. As she turned away from the gruesome sight, Astari grabbed her shoulders, and pulled Essie's back to her chest. She circled her waist with a rigid arm. The cold steel of the gold knife pressed at Essie's throat. Its sharp edge slipped against her already broken skin, stinging like a papercut.

'So, here's the choice before you, Doctor Essie. Help me use the Time Weaver, and as a mercy to you, I will let your friends live out what remains of their cursed lives while they still have time. But history will change. I will change it by eliminating the Amaranthine.'

Essie tried to steady her breath and stop herself from shaking, conscious of the knife flush to her neck.

'It doesn't work like that, Astari. I tried to rewrite the past by stopping my parents' accident. But the same thing happened again. I don't fully understand it, but the force of time seems to compensate for our actions. It's like a river when you throw a rock into it. The displaced water just finds a new path. I don't think we can rewrite the past.'

Astari stilled. The blade shifted away from Essie, and Astari's grip relaxed. Maybe she was listening. Maybe she would see sense. But then suddenly, her hold tightened, and the knife was on Essie's skin again.

'All right, I'll go back to the source of the damn river then. We'll return to when the humans created the first

Amaranthine. I'll cut off Frankenstein's monster at the root. There has to be a way to end this and make sure it never happens again.'

David dragged himself upright and climbed onto his knees, shaking with the effort. Astari turned her gaze on him and narrowed her eyes, concentrating. He dropped back onto all fours, his breaths ragged, sweat beading his forehead. Essie's stomach clenched.

'There is another way,' he panted. 'Let us help you, Astari. Raf and I can help you.'

She gave a bitter laugh and Essie shivered as her hot breath hit the back of her neck.

'Rafael? Look at him! That's what happens when you've been reverting too long. Why would I want to wait for that to happen to me?'

She willed Rafael to move. To do anything. They wouldn't be able to get out of this without him.

Please be okay. Please get up.

'And you! How can *you* help me? You hide behind your vows and your noble sentiment. You deny what you want because you're terrified you'll never be enough for her.'

Astari squeezed harder, and the blade burned against Essie's throat. David placed one foot on the ground and tried to hoist himself up again, only to crumble. Whatever mind control Astari was using on him, he didn't seem to be able to break free.

Despair washed over her. She fought to keep herself from trembling. If Astari's plan worked and she killed off the Amaranthine, the consequences were difficult to predict. But she suspected it wouldn't be good. The

Amaranthine had fought to keep the Bloodborns in check for centuries. Without them . . .

'I won't help you do this, Astari. I can't.'

'I thought you might not want to cooperate willingly. So, I took out insurance by feeding you some of Anna's blood.'

Essie ran her tongue around her lips and tasted it. The coppery bitterness of blood. That was the odd flavour in her mouth. Nausea rose in her throat again.

'If I kill you with Anna's blood in your system, you know what that means. You'll become one of them. And you'll be *dying* to help me then. You'll even help me dispose of your Amaranthine friends. Permanently.'

Astari lowered the knife and shoved her towards David, still gripping her painfully by the shoulders.

'If she's one of them, you know you'll be forced to kill her yourself. Can you really do that?'

David raised his head. At the closer distance, she could see how much pain he was in. Sweat beaded across his brow, his body contorted and strained. Rafael still lay unmoving. He wasn't going to be able to help them. If he was even still alive. Her father was probably dead too. And there was no one else. No one was coming to save them.

David winced as he finally staggered to his feet, still hunched over.

'Please don't hurt her.'

His voice was quiet, pleading. A crack opened in her heart.

'Why not?' Astari snarled.

'You know why,' he replied softly. But he wasn't

looking at Astari. He held Essie's eyes with his own. His beautiful, ever-changing eyes. They were the colour of a grey-green sea one minute and then as dark as a midnight sky the next. They held the warmth and affection of the gentlest man she'd ever known, but also the strength and conviction of a warrior. Those eyes made her feel seen. They made the world a place where she actually wanted to exist. Even if knowing him meant that the world was also full of vampires and monsters. Even if it was still a world where there were no guarantees. No safe passage. It was worth the risk, worth the pain, because at least he was in it.

He has to be in this world.

Like a whisper, the truth stole over her soul, leaving her breathless. She felt for Cecil's bicycle charm, and her hand closed over it.

I can't be an island anymore.

Even if it hurts sometimes, it's worth it.

A sad smile tugged at the corners of her mouth. It was an inconvenient moment to have an emotional revelation. There really could not have been a worse time for her to finally understand what was happening. To finally feel without being afraid. To finally know, with both her head and her heart, that there was something she wanted more than protecting herself, more than simply staying safe.

But there wasn't much she could do about it now. At least this new knowledge made her next steps easy.

Clarity burst into her brain like an explosion of light. Astari had already alluded to the most logical answer.

If I become a Bloodborn, he'll be forced to kill me.

She'd be an easy mark. He'd said that newborn vampires were vulnerable. She had no idea how to fight. And it would create a distraction, hopefully throw Astari off her mind control. If David wasn't in pain, then he could move quickly enough to take both her and Astari down before the Time Weaver could be used. She would die. But Astari would be stopped. The fabric of time would remain intact and all the Amaranthine would be safe.

David will be safe.

'David, listen,' she whispered. 'Maybe Astari's right. Maybe this does need to end.' She dropped the bicycle charm and gently clutched the knife. With shaking hands, she raised it against her throat. He understood instantly what she was planning. A look of horror fell over his face. He staggered towards her.

'Essie ... don't.'

'It's the logical thing to do. You know that I'm right.'

'See,' Astari said. 'I told you she'd betray you.'

Astari's accusation stung, but she held David's gaze.

'Logic is not always the answer.' He took another swaying step, his knees trembling.

'No. I know.' A smile quirked one corner of her mouth. 'You were right about that. You said that logic is a compass, it can guide us, but it can't guarantee us safe passage. I asked you what does. I wanted to know how to keep myself safe. Safe from the pain of living. You didn't get the chance to answer me. But I think I've worked it out on my own.'

She swallowed and squeezed the knife. One edge of the blade was against her palm, the other against her throat. Astari shifted, closing her hand over the knife as well, pressing into Essie's back for better leverage. Essie took a steadying breath, her legs heavy.

'The truth is that nothing can guarantee our safety. When we risk ourselves, there are never any guarantees. But we should take the risk anyway. I didn't really understand that before. Maybe I do now . . .'

She broke off, pressing her eyes closed as she remembered her parents.

'No, Essie, not this. No . . .'

His voice was a strangled cry echoing in the silence of the library. She kept her eyes shut. There was no way she could look at him and do it. If she looked at him again, she'd break. She kept the vision of him in her mind as she sucked air into her lungs. Maybe for the last time. Slowly, she clasped both her hands around the blade at her throat and tensed her arms, preparing to pull it towards her neck.

'I'm sorry, David,' she whispered. 'Please be quick.'

Then the earth tilted, and she was falling.

Chapter 27

David

The pounding pressure abruptly ceased and David's hand dropped from his forehead. Astari's focus was on Essie pulling the knife. She had lost her concentration on him. As the pain started easing off, Essie's words resurfaced in his mind.

Nothing can guarantee our safety.

But we should take the risk anyway.

Her knees wobbled together and she smiled at him, but the smile didn't touch her eyes. She wouldn't do it, would she? She wouldn't drag that knife across her throat and let herself become a Bloodborn? In the church when they fought Sabine, she had sliced her finger open to draw the vampires to her, creating a distraction. And it had worked. Of course she would do it again. He'd be forced to kill her and she'd be taken out of the equation. Astari wouldn't be able to use the Time Weaver. It was biologically imprinted to Essie alone. If she was dead, it was useless.

But he couldn't let that happen.

Steeling himself, he pushed up onto his feet. The pressure was gone, but the pain had stripped his strength. His vision was blurry and his arms and legs moved like lead. He swung his head towards Raf, but his body was still prone beneath the bookshelf. He took a trembling step, then faltered. How was he going to prevent her from doing this?

The doors to the library burst open and the air shifted. He wiped the sweat from his eyes, but he still couldn't be sure exactly what he was seeing.

Gilbert?

Essie's father ran across the room, charging towards Astari. He was slow, even for a human, but his eyes were focussed and determined. He raised something bright and solid over his head. A fire extinguisher. He gripped the hose in his hand and squeezed. A cloud of white powder blasted it into Astari's face. Blindsided, she moved to counter his attack. Essie was flung aside. The gold knife clattered to the ground with the Time Weaver, landing near David's feet. Foam spewed out from the fire extinguisher, covering Astari in ashy powder. She stumbled backwards, coughing.

Something shifted inside him, like shackles falling loose. He took an open breath, his lungs expanding to capacity. Climbing to his feet, his body extended to its full height. Energy flooded his muscles like a dam wall releasing water, flowing out to his fingertips and toes. All his senses awakened with renewed vitality. He flexed his arms and narrowed his eyes.

Astari's eyelids fluttered, trying to clear the residue from her eyes. He lunged for her gold knife. Despite the blinding effects of the fire retardant, she anticipated his movement and beat him to it with her superior speed. Gripping the knife in both hands, she slashed at him blindly. He grimaced as the tip of the blade grazed the skin on his arm. Then Astari fell back again.

'Argh!' She clawed at her eyes wildly, tearing away flesh. Tears gushed down her cheeks as she fell to the floor, thrashing about, a wraithlike spectre with her powder-white face. David flicked the knife upwards with the toe of his boot, catching it by the hilt. As Astari lay prone before him, he waivered. He had never relished killing. Not when he was a soldier and not now, even when it came to killing Bloodborns. But protecting the humans was the reason for his very existence. It was his vow. And what other punishment was possible? He couldn't arrest Astari or imprison her. She was too much of a threat to let go. There was only one way to end it.

'Last chance, Astari. Let us help you or . . .'

'Or what?' she hissed. Her body trembled violently and her face contorted. 'Do it! End this now! Please.'

She jerked into a ball, sobbing. David looked for Essie. Gilbert was standing beside her, his arm around her shoulders. He unclenched his jaw. She was safe. They both were.

An unexpected sting pierced his ankle, penetrating straight through muscle and sinew. He gasped as he collapsed to his knees. Astari raised herself up, another tiny, jewelled dagger in her hand. Gilbert leapt onto her back, throwing his full weight at her. Essie followed her father's lead, her arms encircling Astari's legs. Pummeled by them both, she fell face forwards to the ground. David acted reflexively, slicing through the air with the golden knife. He brought it down on her pale throat with one fluid stroke. Her severed head rolled to the side, eyelids closed. Gilbert and Essie fell back, both panting. He let out a tense breath as he lowered the knife, relief coursing through him.

A low moan came from beneath the toppled bookshelf.

'Raf!'

David regained his feet. His wounds were not too serious and already beginning to heal. He picked his way through the fallen books to where his friend was lying, trapped. Gripping the edge of the shelf, he eased it back upright, freeing Raf's head and torso. He lay there silently, face to the ground. A moment passed, and David tensed. Then he rolled onto his back, his chest heaving, his eyes glinting. David's shoulders fell, relief coursing through him.

'What happened to you? I thought you were going to create a distraction?'

Raf frowned.

'It was bad timing for human moment. I fell. I did not hear her coming. She struck me with something heavy. I woke up inside cupboard.'

Raf touched the side of his face gingerly. Where a wound should have been, there was barely a bruise. David released a sigh and bent over, resting his hands on his knees as he looked for Essie again. She was still kneeling next to her father, a handkerchief pressed to her throat.

'Are you all right?'

She nodded. 'I'm fine. It's just a scratch.'

He glanced around. Books of all shapes and colours lay everywhere. White foam bubbled around them. Spots of blood stained the carpet. But all things considered, it was a pretty good outcome. And it was over. It was finally all over. They had found Gilbert, the Bloodborns were dead, and so was their accomplice. Essie and Rafael were safe. It was finally time to go home.

By the time they had tidied the library and tried to erase all evidence of the events that had taken place at the high school, it was mid-morning. As the car sped up the highway back towards the city, David kept glancing in the rearview mirror, hoping their stolen vehicle wouldn't be pulled over by the police. It would be difficult enough to explain why there was a headless corpse in the boot of the car, let alone that the corpse was not human.

Essie sat quietly in the passenger seat beside him. She hadn't said much since they got in the car. He worried she was in shock, or worse, now that she had seen him behead a woman, she would never speak to him again.

'I'm sorry you had to see that – what I did. I . . . I didn't want to kill her . . .' He kept his eyes on the road, unable to bring himself to see her reaction.

She reached across the car and covered his hand with hers. The warmth of her touch sent a vibration up his arm.

'It wasn't your fault. You tried to help her, but she would have killed us and tried to kill all the Amaranthine. You were protecting us. We all trusted her.'

David nodded as he met Raf's dark eyes in the rearview mirror. Astari's duplicity sat like a hard lump in his stomach. There was much for them to discuss. He had always thought the Amaranthine vow was paramount. That's what Raf had taught him. He realised now that he had also assumed it made them immune to compromise. But Astari had betrayed that vow. She had caused the death of her progeny. She was prepared to turn a human into a Bloodborn and hunt the rest of the Amaranthine through time. Was that what their joint dreams of the dead Amaranthine had been alluding to? Or was there still more to come? They needed to discover who had delivered the note and the treacherous golden knife to Astari. He couldn't shake the feeling that someone was playing the long game. The figure in the dark hood kept coming back into his mind.

But the thought that left him even more uneasy was that it was mostly betrayal at the hands of a human that had driven Astari's actions. Raf's warnings about being involved with mortals echoed in his ears in a fresh way. He moved his hand from underneath Essie's and gripped the steering wheel.

'Why did you try to get yourself killed, Essie?'

She huffed in response, folding her arms over her chest.

'It was the only way out. She would have hunted all the Amaranthine, including you. I had to.'

'I would have found another way.'

She shrugged. 'You didn't need to.'

'Do you know what it would have done to me if I . . . if I had to do that?'

She was silent. He couldn't look at her.

'Anna's blood will pass from your system within twenty-four hours or so. You should be fine.'

'All right.' She twisted in her seat. 'Dad, you were incredible! You came from nowhere!'

Gilbert frowned. 'It's hard to describe, but it was like waking up from a terrible nightmare. I remember falling through the wormhole. I remember meeting Astari, and then it was like a black fog came over my mind. I couldn't think clearly. I was in a waking dream all the time. I couldn't tell what was real or sort out past from the present. Then suddenly, the fog lifted. I remembered everything. And I remembered I needed to protect Essie. I needed to help her.'

'That was Astari's fault, Dad. She was able to use some kind of mind control. At least it doesn't seem to have done any permanent damage.'

David was still getting used to this new Gilbert who looked you in the eye and answered questions lucidly. A man who seemed fully present. The man, the father, that Essie had once known. But in the rearview mirror, David could see that his aged features were still etched with guilt. He couldn't say he truly trusted him. Not yet. But he was happy for Essie that he seemed to be recovering. In time, maybe she would get him back completely. And maybe that would be for the best. Maybe that was what she needed most. Normal human connections. A life without blood and chaos. A life without him in it.

Chapter 28

Essie

The sun was bright and the sky clear again after the summer storm of the night before. Following the intense rain, everything smelled new and fresh. Essie's eyes had closed briefly on the trip back to the city, but the adrenaline spike of nearly having her throat slashed was still buzzing through her body. She knew she wouldn't feel fully relaxed until they were all safely back in their present. Even then, it might take a while. She touched the Time Weaver on her wrist, feeling the smooth face. Luckily, it still seemed intact after the scuffle when Astari had dropped it.

David glanced over at her.

'You're awake.' He turned the car into a parking lot. She stretched and looked around. If she had to guess, she'd say they were probably a few blocks from the alley where they had arrived in the past only three days earlier. Three days that felt like a lifetime.

'All right, this is the end of the road.' David eased on

the handbrake but left the car running. She gave him a questioning look.

'I need to dispose of that.' He nodded meaningfully towards the back of the car. 'There's an incinerator at the industrial site back on the edge of the city. I'll leave the car there as well.'

'Oh,' she said.

'I won't be long.'

She undid her seatbelt and waited for Gilbert and Rafael to get out of the back of the car.

'So, you'll meet us there – in the alley where we arrived? Mum said . . .'

Her eyes watered and David reflexively patted his pockets for his handkerchief. They both laughed as she drew one of his out of her own jacket. She dabbed at her eyes and inhaled a deep breath.

'Mum mentioned that the geographical location could be a bit off with the Time Weaver, so I think it's best if we leave from the same place we arrived. That way, hopefully, we'll end up back in my lounge room in our present, and not say, in the path of an oncoming train.'

'I agree,' he said solemnly, his face deadpan. 'Death by train would be a sad way to go, after everything we have survived.'

Her eyes widened at him. 'That's not funny.' She slapped him lightly. He caught her hand and held it, pressing it gently to his chest. Her eyes met his as a ray of sunshine spilled over the dashboard. He squinted into the light as it hit his face. A sheen of perspiration glistened on his forehead. She frowned.

'Are you sure you're feeling okay now?'

'Oh,' he said as he wiped at his forehead with the back of his hand. 'I am feeling better. The headaches – they've stopped. Now that Astari's . . . gone.'

'That's good.'

She opened the car door and hopped out then turned and leaned on the open windowsill.

'This is almost all over. We get to go home now.'

He nodded, but his brow creased. 'When we get back, we need to talk.'

A feeling of apprehension stole over her.

'Okay.' She tried to keep her response light.

'I'll see you soon.'

He revved the engine. As she pushed off the door, he turned the car around and drove out of the carpark.

She followed her father and Rafael down the street towards the alley. Her father asked so many questions as they walked. How had Rhonda found them? How had she travelled to the future to find Essie? Did Rhonda know she was going to die in a car accident? Why hadn't Essie been able to stop it? She tried to be patient with him. She knew he had been through a lot, and miraculously, now he seemed to be returning to his senses. But everything was still so raw for her. Her mother's death. Her conflicting emotions about her father and what he had done. His betrayal, and now, repentance. And there was still so much of the science she didn't understand yet.

'I tried to stop the accident, and it happened anyway. Do you remember? You were there with me?'

He scratched his head. 'I remember the dark road at night. But it was like a dream. I don't know.'

She smiled tightly. 'It's all right. Give yourself some time. Things will probably start coming back.'

'So, the past version of me, I'm at the hospital now with you – eight-year-old you – after the accident?'

A shiver ran down her back. She remembered waking up in the hospital all those years ago. A scared little girl, in pain, the future so uncertain. She shrugged, trying to re-anchor herself in the present moment.

'I guess. But you are also here with me now. Thirty-two-year-old me.'

His face folded with lines of sadness. He was obviously having trouble coping. She hadn't taken it all in either. Maybe she never would.

'Try to focus on here and now, Dad. We have to go home, back to our own time. Things will seem better from there.' She hoped her words would be true.

He nodded uncertainly. It was a lot. Everything was a lot. For all of them. Except maybe Rafael. He was his usual taciturn self. But she could tell from the slant of his grey-black eyebrows, the lift of his chin, something was bothering him. He had been betrayed by Astari too. And she knew he had liked Astari. She was his equal in many ways, in a world where everyone else, especially humans, must seem so small and insignificant with their fleeting lives. And she knew he would see what had happened with Astari as yet more proof of the perils of vampire-human relationships. Humans were to be protected, but not trusted. Neither, it seemed, were all the Amaranthine. Astari's relationship with a human had eventually driven her to do terrible things. Was that what Rafael feared? Was that something David worried about too?

The smell of fresh coffee caught her attention and made her stomach complain. She couldn't even remember the last time she had eaten something decent.

'I need food.'

She dragged her father towards the coffee scent. A man in overalls passed her on his way out, greasy takeaway food in hand. She went to the counter to order, then remembered again that she had no money. The woman behind the counter stared at her and the drama of being taken to the police station flashed back.

Dharma.

She pictured his boyish face, smelt the cigarettes on his skin, and closed her eyes against the memory. It was too soon. She tried to think about something else, but it winded her for a moment. She stumbled to one of the café chairs and slumped down.

'What's wrong, Ess?' Her father sat down beside her.

She looked into his eyes and tried to find the words to describe the emotions that were swirling inside her, the sense of overwhelm at everything that had happened, and how she still hadn't had time to process it. At least they were all safe now. She'd be back with David soon.

'I forgot we don't have any money, Dad.' She gave a short laugh. 'I can't buy us breakfast. Sorry. Can you wait a bit longer?'

He dug around in his pockets. He unfurled his palm revealing a handful of gold coins. The change from the taxi ride. It wasn't much, maybe ten dollars, but it would be enough to get a couple of hot drinks and a muffin.

'Us oldies always carry loose change around in our pockets.' He winked at her.

She smiled at him as she took the money and went back to the counter. The waitress took her order and brought them tea in takeaway cups and a raspberry muffin. Rafael stood waiting outside the café door, like some ancient sentinel, back straight, eyes scanning the horizon. She wondered briefly if he ever rested from his mission.

'Come.' He beckoned them. 'You eat and walk. *Dado* will be there soon.'

As they rounded the corner to the alley, the city seemed to come to life with the midday lunch break. Cars crowded the roads, pedestrians marched along, briefcases in hands, newspapers curled under arms. She thought about how different it would be in the not-so-distant future. In a few decades, people would walk the streets with their heads buried in tiny palm-sized devices that held the world, not just local news. They would be able to shut out the sounds of life around them with micro speakers nestled inside their ears. And none of them had any idea yet. Was that how it felt to be like David or Rafael? Did the passage of so much time always seem like mere moments to them?

Her heart sped up when she saw him there, already waiting. He was leaning against the brick building on the left of the alley, arms folded over his chest, one leg bent behind him to brace himself. He looked immaculate and respectable. His hair was combed against his head and his suit was a little worse for wear, but still neat. He did not look at all like a man who had just incinerated a headless body, nor a vampire detective who was over one hundred years old. As they approached, he pushed off the wall, revealing a white paper bag in his hand.

'Oh good, you're eating. I thought you'd forget. Here you go. Have more to eat.'

He handed her a bag. She opened it to find another muffin. A warm feeling curled in her stomach as well.

She split the second muffin with her father and they gratefully finished it.

Rafael glanced up and down the alley nervously. The sun was rising higher in the sky. They were still alone, but maybe not for long.

'All right. Is time.'

She drew a deep breath and nodded. So much had changed in the last few days, and yet everything would stay the same. Or it should. In theory, when they got home, it would be like they had never left. Moffatt would be there waiting for her in her cosy, familiar lounge room. She peeled back her shirt sleeve and adjusted the settings on the Time Weaver to the day and time they had left. Taking her father's hand, the four of them moved into a circle formation, just as they had done with her mother days before. Her father eyed her carefully, his face concerned.

'Don't worry, Dad. I promise everything will be all right.'

She double checked the settings and pressed the activation button. The little blue lights ticked over in sequence while the atmosphere around them changed. She took one last look, trying to imprint the details on her memory forever. The light morphed into a circular rainbow again and started to gather speed. Rubbish in the alley lifted and swirled with the rainbow. Then the roaring noise surrounded them.

'Close your eyes, Dad.'

Her father gripped her hand firmly, and she held onto David's. Her chest swooped as she fell backwards, anchored through time to the future, an invisible thread, pulling them all home.

Chapter 29

Essie

'I check everything,' Rafael announced as he headed up the stairs. The house looked undisturbed to Essie and David said it was fine. But the older vampire couldn't help himself it seemed.

She whirled around in a circle, taking in every detail of her little home. It felt like she had been gone three months, not three days. And yet, she had also been gone no time at all. It would take a while to comprehend that. And everything else that they had been through. But for now, she just wanted to enjoy it. She sank onto her couch and sighed contentedly.

Moffatt meowed and nudged her father's leg. He leaned down and patted the cat's soft head.

'Who's this then?'

'It's a long story.'

'Right, well how about I make us some tea and you can tell me about it?' he said cheerily. Her heart lifted. How long had she wanted to hear him offering to make her something as simple as a cup of tea?

'That sounds great, Dad.'

'Back in a jiffy then.' He disappeared into the kitchen, and she smiled.

David was leaning against the wall, his head tilted to the side, watching her.

'It's good to see you smile,' he said.

'I'm glad to be home. All of us safe. It feels like a miracle.'

He nodded, but she could sense he was weighing his next words.

'We need to talk.' He moved over to the couch and sat beside her.

'You mentioned earlier. About what though?'

'About what's next.'

She froze.

What was next? Next for them? In her old high school library, under the threat of Astari's knife, she had been one hundred percent sure how she felt. She didn't want to be an island. But she was still uncertain about what the implications of that were. All the *feelings stuff* was so hard and murky. She knew she'd need time to figure it out. But he was looking at her now, his eyes expectant.

'I . . . I . . . um.'

'You have a ball this week, don't you?'

Her shoulders relaxed and simultaneously a sense of disappointment fell on her. He meant what was next, as in next *on her calendar*.

'Yes. It's a new fundraising thing. All the Board

members will be there. We're supposed to go and schmooze with them so they will give us more money for the Institute. I'd rather stick pins in my eyes, but I do want to be there for the presentation of the new scholarship in Cecil's memory. Plus, attendance is mandated in my employment contract, according to Angela.'

David nodded. 'I see.'

'I'm allowed to bring a guest. It's not the dinner date we talked about, but it would be way more fun with you there. Do you have a tux?' She grinned as she envisioned him in a smart black and white version of his everyday attire.

'I think I probably do somewhere.'

His voice was flat, and he didn't return her smile. There was something in his eyes she didn't recognise. He loosened his tie.

'But I don't know if it's a good idea for me to go.'

'Okay.' She looked away, focussing her gaze on anything else as the heat raced to her cheeks. She replayed the moment he had touched her face in the motel room. Had she imagined it all? Was it just in her mind?

'It's not that I don't want to,' he followed up quickly.

Her eyes were drawn back to his. His face had softened, the lines around his forehead smoothed out. She noticed his brow was shining with tiny beads of perspiration again. He shrugged off his jacket and hung over it the back of the couch. She sat forwards in alarm.

'What's that?' she said, pointing at a red stain spreading across his shirt sleeve.

He inspected it, as if noticing the wound for the first time.

'Oh. I think Astari nicked me when we fought.'

He peeled his shirt sleeve back, and she had to resist the urge to recoil. The cut was an angry, red stripe that extended past his elbow. He turned his arm over. Bluish tendrils snaked their way out from the cut over his pale flesh. She swallowed hard before she forced a laugh.

'Why hasn't it healed?'

He didn't respond. He stood up, and she did too.

'Maybe you need food. You're always pestering me to eat, but when was the last time you fed?'

'Raf!'

His voice was low, urgent.

Rafael appeared instantaneously, causing her to take a step back in his wake. He tore David's sleeve out of the way. The bluish lines went all the way up to his biceps. The two vampires exchanged a meaningful look and a queasy feeling gathered in the pit of her stomach. She shook her head. It was a cut, not even a very deep one. David obviously needed to feed, and he would get better. The same way he did after the Bloodborn in her house practically shattered his spine. The same way he did in the church, after Sabine impaled him, crushed his eye socket and ripped his chest open. All those injuries had been far worse than this. This was just a cut. She rolled up her own sleeve impatiently.

'Here,' she said, extending her forearm to him and forcing another hollow laugh.

'No.'

David's voice was like gravel. Rafael angled himself between her and David and pushed her behind him defensively.

'What's wrong?'

Her voice was shaking. The trembling spread to her body. The feeling in her stomach bloomed and knotted. She already knew the answer. Still, her mind fought it.

It can't be.

It's not.

'Stay away from me.' He pulled down his sleeve and turned his back on them.

This is not happening.

It can't be happening.

We're all safe now.

'Come, Essie.' Rafael took her by the arm.

She snatched it away. 'Talk to me, both of you. Tell me what is going on!'

'Raf, now!'

David's hands gripped his head as he spun around. When his eyes swung back to her, the air flew from her lungs. His face was pale and contorted, his cheeks hollow. And his eyes. God, his eyes. They weren't a soothing blue or iridescent green. The irises were black and ringed with crimson, like a Bloodborn. And they were filled with . . . disgust. He'd never looked at her like that before.

'David,' she whispered, reaching for him. He flinched like she'd hit him, and in a blur, he disappeared up the stairs. Strong arms encircled her waist and almost lifted her from her feet, pulling her backwards.

'Raf, please! Let me go!'

But Rafael held her in place as she sobbed, his arms as unmoving as stone.

'You have seen this before. We both have.'

Ugly visions of Dharma hit her fiercely, nearly doubling her over.

'But how is that possible? When? How could it have happened?'

She shuddered, remembering how Astari had showed them the special hilt of her knife, the way it stored infected blood. She must have used it on him when they fought.

Rafael steered her to the couch and set her down.

'We have to help him. We have to find a cure.'

His dark eyes clouded over, and he dropped his gaze.

'There is no cure. You know this.'

She threw up her arms.

'There has to be! We'll do some research. We'll take him to a biochemist for tests. Bloodrot is transmitted by blood – it must be some kind of viral blood infection. We could try antibiotics? Something? Anything?'

He shook his head. 'Humans may discover what he is. Our vows . . .'

'Screw your bloody vows!'

She was trembling with anger and something else she couldn't name.

'He's your friend, Rafael. He's my . . . my . . . we have to do *something*! We can't just let him end up like Dharma. We can't. I won't let that happen to him.'

Rafael turned away. He leaned forwards with his elbows on his knees, his hand bristling across his chin.

'Please, Rafael.' She slid to the floor and knelt before

him. 'If there's anything we can do – anything – we have to try. What about the story you mentioned?'

He worked his jaw, hesitating.

'That was legend Nika mentioned once. I don't know details.'

'What do you remember?' She leaned towards him intently, her face level with his.

'Her sire, Aleksander, talked of cure.'

She pushed her glasses up her nose, her eyes still intent on him.

'And?'

'Nothing more. I did not ask. Was not important at time.'

She lifted her wrist, which still had the Time Weaver wrapped around it.

'We can go back and ask Nika now.'

Rafael scowled.

'When we travel to your past – twenty or so years – that is one thing. Nika lived centuries ago. And maybe she not know more than what I tell you.'

Essie cupped his calloused hands in hers. He flinched at her touch, but she held on. She was prepared to beg if that was what it took.

'This might be his only hope. You love him. I know you do. And I . . .'

Even now, the words stuck on her tongue. She cleared her throat.

'He's done so much for me. If there's a way to help him, I have to try.'

One corner of his mouth lifted. He sighed heavily.

'All right. We try. But first, we must make arrangements. He cannot be left alone. He is already danger to humans and will only become more dangerous.'

'Yes. Anything. We'll do whatever we have to do to keep him and everyone else safe. But remember, we can leave and return in practically the same moment. Even if we are gone for months, it would be less than an hour for him.'

'That is good thing. You saw how quickly Dharma succumbed. *Dado* does not have long.'

The kitchen door swung open and her father backed into the room, balancing a tray with a teapot and tea cups. She sat back on her heels.

'What's going on? Who doesn't have long?'

He looked expectantly between her and Rafael. She caught Rafael's eye, giving him a questioning look. He nodded slightly.

'I don't have time to explain everything, but David is sick. Rafael and I need to go away again to find some medicine for him. And we need your help to take care of him while we're gone.'

Her father placed the tray down on the coffee table in front of them.

'Of course, whatever you need. It's the least I can do after how he has helped us.'

Was she really going to do this again? Could she trust her father with something so dangerous and important? Was there any other choice?

Moffatt meowed, sidling up to her leg. She patted his soft head and scratched his neck.

'Oh little Moff, I'm sorry, but I have to go again. Don't worry. I'll be back before you know it.'

The cat purred his satisfaction for a moment, then suddenly skittered away, ducking beneath the couch. A deep growl sounded from the stairs sending a shiver through the air. Essie whirled around as David lunged towards her. His incisors were distended and razor sharp, and his eyes blazed like fire, swirling with all the colours of a blood moon.

Read on for a sneak peek at the next book in this series.

Chapter 1

David

The calf was born in the depths of winter, slick with afterbirth, legs trembling too much to stand. David knelt beside it, shivering in his thin coat, his breath a mist in the air.

'Lina, get water, clean towels!' His little sister stood on her spindly legs and ran towards their cottage. But by the time she returned, the barn was too quiet. The calf lay still. The mother lay beside it, nudging it with her nose. It did not move. There was faint steam rising from its cooling body. David dropped to his knees. Pressed his hand against its tiny chest. Nothing. No beat. No breath.

Lina set the towel and water down beside him.

'Is it sleeping?'

He moved his head slowly from side to side. He couldn't meet her eyes.

Then the barn door slammed open.

A storm of movement. Their father – his coat dripping with rain and fury. One look at the calf and the colour drained from his face.

'What have you done?'

Rigours seized David and he became conscious again, attempting to breathe through the agony that wracked his body with every spasm. He clawed at his hair in vain, trying to rip the memory from his brain. How could that cursed scene be so achingly clear in his mind after all this time? Things he thought he had concealed in the past. So many things he had fought to forget. The thirst in the back of his throat smouldered, embers waiting for a breeze to spark them to life. He writhed against the manacles holding his hands over his head as his body became a pincushion. A thousand tiny holes opened up in his skin – the bloodrot rioting through his veins. Despite the pain, he sighed, relieved.

It was just a dream.

But when would his waking nightmare ever end?

It was almost entirely dark where he was now, locked in the attic room of Rafael's flat. But he squeezed his eyes shut against the minuscule shafts of light breaking through the heavily curtained window high on the wall opposite him. Any skerrick of sun felt like knives through his irises. As his tremors slowly petered out, he exhaled a long breath and tried to relax his muscles. Whenever he tensed his shoulders, it made the wound on his arm feel worse. He shifted his position, trying to get comfortable with his back against the cold stone wall where he was chained up for everyone's safety. It was fortunate that

Rafael had prepared such a place. He said he had built it in case they ever needed to restrain a Bloodborn. Ironic it was now *him* needing restraint.

He wasn't sure how long it had been since the bloodrot symptoms started. Essie noticed it first. The sweating. Then the blooming infection. The dark blue veins lining his skin like tattoos had spread over most of his body now. The virus was taking hold. Though he couldn't determine the exact timeline, he felt sure he had been sick long enough that he would enter the paralysis phase soon. Or maybe that was just what he hoped for. It meant he would be closer to death, but at least the rigours would end. And the visions of his past . . .

Dharma had seemed more peaceful when the paralysis set in.

Dharma.

Astari.

More death. More failure. He squeezed his eyes shut against their memories and swallowed hard, trying to quench his parched throat. That was the worst part of the physical symptoms – the urge that never went away. The endless, mindless thirst for blood. As an Amaranthine, he had drunk blood. It was hideous, but necessary. His half-vampire body required it for sustenance in the same way humans needed water. But he had never craved it. Never been a slave to it. Not like the Bloodborns.

Now, blood was so much more. Blood remembered. Blood weaved together the story of every human life. It carried memory – instinct, hunger, love. It was the beginning and the end of every impulse. It was life itself.

And he *needed* it.

It wasn't like how humans needed water. That analogy was wholly inadequate. This was something else. Something transcendent.

Over the last hours or days, he wasn't sure how long, Essie had researched bloodrot, talked to contacts in her scientific circles who knew more about biology, but no one had heard of a blood disease like this. And of course, she couldn't be forthcoming with any blood samples or other biological information from him. That was out of the question.

A soft knock on the attic door caused him to raise his head. He smelt her before he could see her.

'You shouldn't be here.' He hated the sound of his voice. Rough and calloused.

'I brought you this.' She stepped into the gloom of the attic. Tearing the seal of the blood bag in her hand, she knelt before him and held the straw-like tube to his lips. He flinched away from her. The shackles securing his hands over his head clanged together against the bricks.

'You shouldn't be here,' he repeated, closing his lips in a tight line. Images flashed through his mind. He remembered bearing down on her, her face a mask of horror as Rafael peeled him away, barely restraining him from trying to rip out her throat.

'I attacked you. I would have killed you if not . . . if not . . .'

'You have to drink this. It will make you feel better and buy us a little more time.'

She shoved the tube at his lips, forcing the straw into

his mouth. As she squeezed the bag, the contents flowed over his tongue. For a moment, there was the sweet bliss of a reprieve, but it was mercilessly short-lived. He drained the bag in seconds and immediately his throat began to ache again. The sound of Essie's living heart, its fevered drumbeat, resounded inside his head. The pulse at her neck bounced softly. He could almost see the blood moving through her veins. Shuddering with revulsion, he turned his head away from her.

'You shouldn't be here.'

'I am about to go,' she replied, her tone matter-of-fact. 'Rafael and I need to get geographically closer to the place where we can find Nika. We're flying out to Rome in an hour.'

He shook his head weakly. Since Essie had not been able to discover anything through her research, she and Rafael had come up with a plan to save his immortal life. Time travelling to the past to undo Astari's actions in infecting him in the first place was pointless. They'd figured that out when Essie had tried to save her mother from the car accident. But they could travel to Italy, and then to the distant past to find Nika, and ask her about the myth of Nanshe's blood. Gilbert would stay to watch over him, feed him regular blood bags, and make sure he remained chained in the attic.

It was a plan that was both foolish and dangerous for everyone involved. And it was completely unnecessary.

David had resigned himself to his fate. He wasn't afraid to die, and he had few regrets. There were some things he wished he had done or said. Things he might have told Essie if they'd had longer. But even that was probably for the best. The way events had unfolded, she could go on living a normal life and not have to be part of his dark and confronting world. Rafael would keep an eye on her, make sure there was no more Bloodborn trouble. She'd experienced enough of that for one human lifetime. After everything she had been through, she deserved a chance at happiness. Ordinary human happiness.

But instead, she and Rafael were both putting themselves at risk for him. It was intolerable. He was a lost cause. They all knew it. They'd all been there when Dharma succumbed to bloodrot. The least they could do for him now would be to stay safe and live on. Not venture off on a dangerous mission to the past for what was in all likelihood a fool's errand. He hung his head, his chin resting on his chest.

Essie scoffed dryly. 'Stop looking so sorry for yourself, Sorrow. We'll be back before you know it. With answers.'

He raised his weary gaze to her.

'Listen to me, please, Essie. I'm not afraid to die. I was before. The last time. When I went to war, and on that cold night in Skhodra . . . so long ago. But not anymore.'

A smile softened the edge of her mouth and she reached out to touch his cheek. Her hand felt deliciously cool against his burning skin, but he turned his head from her again.

'I know you aren't afraid,' she whispered. 'Courage should be your middle name. That and hope. You always have hope, no matter what.'

He forced a shallow laugh. 'I only said I'm not afraid to die. There are still things I'm afraid of . . .'

'You don't need to be. I'm going to figure this out. Rafael and I will find Nika, and we'll find a way to save you.'

He heard the steel in her voice, her scientist's confidence. But she didn't understand. It wasn't bloodrot or the pain that he feared.

'I don't want you to go. Either of you. It's too great a risk. It's not worth it. I'm not worth it.'

She tilted her head. 'What would you do? If the situation were reversed, would you just give up?'

He dropped his head again and beads of sweat fell onto his lap. A soft, dry cloth dabbed gently at both his temples.

'Don't worry, it's a clean handkerchief. Raf brought a bunch of your things over from your flat.'

She scrunched it up and slipped it into her pocket.

'I'm taking it with me. For luck.'

'I see,' he murmured. 'I thought scientists didn't believe in things like luck. It's not very tangible or measurable.'

Her face broke out in a proper smile.

'If the last few months with you has taught me anything, it's that the world is more complicated and incredible than I had ever imagined. I'm not saying science won't explain it all, one day. But for now, I'll concede that there's room for some mystery, and maybe even a little magic.'

She reached over his head and took hold of one of his manacled hands, giving it a momentary squeeze. Then she straightened and brusquely buttoned her jacket. As she went to leave, his heart clenched as though it was being compressed between heavy weights.

'Ess . . . Esther,' he breathed. She half-turned to face him. 'Please, be safe. Promise me?'

She nodded as she adjusted her glasses. 'I promise.' She flashed him a mischievous grin. 'As long as you promise not to dine on my dad while I'm gone?'

He chuckled at her dark humour despite himself and rattled his safely locked hands. 'Ironclad. Vampire proof. I have no plans other than sitting here in the dark until your return.'

'Good.' She nodded. 'Dad's was eyeing your sword, and I have a feeling he wouldn't mind the chance to try it out. So, it's best you just lie low until I'm back.'

Her eyes lingered on him for a moment longer, then her footsteps receded, and he was alone in the darkness again.

to continue Essie and David's story, read The Shadow and the Mirror

Acknowledgments

Thank you for reading the second book in the Amaranthine Vampires Trilogy. I hope you enjoyed the story. The idea for this book came to me as I was writing the ending for *Blood and Time*. The impetus was partly selfish: I had enjoyed spending time with the characters so much, I didn't want to say goodbye. But I also knew there was still more of David and Essie's story to tell. And as you now know, this book is not the end of the tale either. There's one more book to come to round out the series. Make sure to sign up to my newsletter at www.tpdonohue.com for updates on the release and behind-the-scenes snippets.

Thank you again to my awesome editorial team, Lacey at On the Page Editorial Services, and Cassie at Weaver Way Author Services. I really couldn't have made this story what it is without your expert editorial guidance.

Thank you to my wonderful beta reader team as well: my mum, Colleen, Kate Midena, Ishani Das, Briah McKinnon-Collins, Lara Wood Gladwin, and Caela Gladwin. You all gave time from your busy lives to read early versions of this manuscript and provide invaluable feedback and encouragement.

And thank you to Victoria Cooper for another perfect cover in this series.

Thanks as ever to my family. You have embraced my dream to write wholeheartedly and have always shown me unwavering support. I couldn't do this without you.

And finally, thanks to my God, who has given me life and breath and hope.

About the Author

TP Donohue is an Australian writer who blends fantasy, science fiction and the supernatural. An avid reader, she grew up dreaming of one day sharing her own stories with the world. She is drawn to good coffee, autumn leaves, and an early night. Her short stories have been published in fiction anthologies, and the Amaranthine Vampires Trilogy is her first book series.

Find out more about her books and sign up to be first to receive updates at www.tpdonohuewriter.com.